Call Me Waiter

ALSO BY JOSEPH TORRA

Fiction
Gas Station
Tony Luongo
My Ground
The Bystander's Scrapbook
They Say

Poetry
16 Paintings
Domino Sessions
Keep Watching the Sky
Watteau Sky (with Ed Barrett)
August Letter To My Wife and Daughters
After the Chinese

Call Me Waiter

AN AUTOBIOGRAPHICAL
NOVEL *by* Joseph Torra

2008 : Pressed Wafer : Boston

—Dedicated to all my restaurant friends

Call me Waiter. Or Barkeep. Either one will do. I started this work to put myself through school. Today I gave my notice. During a recent afternoon set-up Betty Ann went to the dish-room and returned with Sammy to kill a fly that'd been buzzing around the new drapes in the front window. It was then I reached an end to my twenty-five year ride. I've done it before. Left a restaurant and sworn the business off forever, only to return.

Betty Ann and her husband Ed are as good as owners get except Barbara and George, owners of the first restaurant I ever worked in Northern New Hampshire. Barbara wouldn't kill a fly—rather shoo it out a window or door. Betty Ann recently returned from a spiritual retreat. She couldn't bring herself to kill that fly.

Sammy had no problem. Six days a week ten hours a day seven years running Sammy works more like a machine than the dish washing machine. Though he speaks little English he'll tell you the name of the band playing any classic rock song on the radio in his dish-room. He sends half his paycheck to his family in El Salvador. His father recently died and on the day he received the news he came to work. In seven years since Tulips opened Sammy never took a vacation but the money instead. This year Ed told him he must take time off it's the law. He rested at home watching television and one of his cousins took over for him during the week. His cousin, glad to have the work, split the week's pay with Sammy.

♦♦♦

In my early twenties I found myself desperate to get out of my hometown of Medford. We had family friends who owned a small restaurant and a motel in the town of Errol, New Hampshire, about two hundred miles north of Boston—not far from the Canadian border. Barbara and George were hard working, loving folks and one time during an overnight visit I expressed dissatisfaction with my situation at home. They invited me up. I could work in the kitchen of the restaurant, draw a small salary and receive free room and board. I could eat free at the restaurant and they gave me a bed in the loft at their home where their two children about my age slept. They had plenty of room and we all got along well.

The Umbagog Restaurant was actually a number of miles from Umbagog Lake in Maine. Errol, New Hampshire is not far from the Maine border and the Umbagog Restaurant, like many local businesses, lakes, ponds and streams carried Native American names. The small restaurant consisted of two counters that met at a right angle. In addition there were four or five tables and a small room attached with a large table and chairs seating up to a dozen. No matter, the place was never full. Most locals ate across the street at the newer and bigger Errol Restaurant operated by the family who owned one of the town's two gas stations, a campground and some prime lots of lakeside property.

Some days I opened which meant rising in the dark, shuffling down the street to start the coffee and pre-cook bacon and home fries. At the time Errol was a lumber town. A few hunters, fisherman and tourists found their way, but without the lumber industry the town couldn't exist. I needed no alarm clock in Errol because by four in the morning the tractor-trailers shifted through their gears rumbling tank-like down the town's main street with the first wood load of the day or were headed back into the woods to pick up the first haul. The drivers stopped in for a coffee and quick order of toast or donut, never much time to sit and enjoy a full breakfast.

After bacon in the oven and home fries on the grill I browned sausages, checked pancake batter and put bread and muffins in order. Once the breakfast was finished I prepped for lunch and dinner. If a turkey or beef needed roasting they went into the oven. I set up the steam tables and made mashed potatoes, stuffing and vegetables like green beans, corn and carrots. During lunch we served cheeseburgers and fries, a hot dog, the occasional hot roast beef or turkey sandwich and the ubiquitous grilled cheese or tuna salad. If I was working the opening shift, I left after lunch around mid-afternoon. The other cook arrived and worked until closing time around eight or nine. The late cook had it better because all the work had been done when he arrived.

◆◆◆

He sends his drink back three times. That's not the record. Sometimes they'll order and don't know what the drink should taste like. You make the drink again. And you make the drink again. There are those who taste wine unaware they taste to detect irregularities. How many fine bottles of wine have been returned in how many restaurants by people who decided they didn't like the wine despite the fact that the wine was fundamentally fine?

Excuse me, Waiter. This dish isn't what I expected.

Oh, I'm sorry to hear that, Sir. Let me get you the menu

and perhaps you can select something to your liking.

The dish goes in the trash or the waiters eat it in the waiter station, the customer makes another selection, we take the first item off the check and I wonder what other business exists where you try a product so that it can't be used again, and if you don't like it you don't pay for it and order another product.

Excuse me is everything to your liking now?

Oh yes fine. Just fine.

♦♦♦

They were simple eaters at the Umbagog. Regulars ordered their usual items. There was a trucker who ate a hamburger and coffee, no matter what time of the day. Another fellow who owned the other gas station in Errol came in every morning ordered raisin toast and coffee. A secretary from the lumber operations office had a cheese sandwich and a coke. One day I made a lasagna and meatball special. Though still somewhat unskilled in the kitchen, I used my mother's recipe as best as I could remember it. It came out delicious. I made a sign and eagerly told all the folks who came in but not one person ordered it so by the second day I realized the locals didn't like food that ended in vowels. When we closed that night Barbara, George, their kids and I sat down in the private room and ate as much lasagna and meatballs as we could.

The only busy time I can recall was during deer hunting season. We opened early and the place filled at five in the morning, still dark outside. The hunters ordered food in vast amounts with extra sides of bacon and ham, mug after mug of coffee and before daybreak the place emptied out as someone dropped their head back and swallowed the last sip of coffee or another rushed out of the men's room pulling up his suspenders, all of them rushing through the door en masse to jeeps and pickups to roar out of the parking lot. Barbara and George's daughter and a friend of hers did much of the waitress work and I was amazed when they told me what they made in tips after one of those hunter rushes.

The same thing happened at dinner when all the hunters returned and ate voraciously as they bragged and lied about their day in the woods. They consumed full dinners of chops and steaks and chicken the likes we might not serve for four or five days running. They devoured pies and cakes a local woman baked and sold to us, her husband was a real trapper. Hunters took apple pies home to the city and spent money like the locals couldn't. And they tipped the girls. It was somewhere around this time it struck me that if there was any money to be made in the business it probably wasn't in the kitchen.

Half way through that winter I got homesick for the city. I made my farewells with the locals and packed my belongings. I asked George to write me a letter of reference. He wrote that I worked at his restaurant in every capacity and found me to be an outstanding employee. I still wasn't certain what I wanted in the business, but something told me a letter of reference might be useful. The next year George and Barbara sold the Umbagog. George told me the best year he ever had he netted a profit of five hundred dollars.

♦♦♦

Back at home during the seventies a lull in the economy made jobs scarce. I took a position at a chain called Bonanza Steak House. The manager took a look at George's letter and my age which was older than most of his employees and offered me an assistant manager position—if I could prove myself.

I washed dishes by day and worked the cook line by night. Bonanza was more like a fast food joint than a steak house. The customer placed the order with the cashier who took the money while verbally transferring the order through a microphone that blared throughout the restaurant on loud speakers so diners and cooks alike were treated to the barrage.

One Bonanza Burger Medium Rare.

One Horse's Cave-Man Steak Rare.

One Little Joe Well Done Extra Mushroom Gravy.

One Adam's Ribs' No Beans.

Two Orders of Texas Toast.

Texas Toast was double-cut slices of white bread cooked on a flat grill with butter. It went on like this all night. To make matters worse it took a customer two or three minutes to gather silverware and tray and pay and when they got to the end of the line the meals weren't always ready. Things got dicey when it was busy and once a biker complained to the manager and when he wasn't satisfied with the response the biker reached over the line and grabbed the manager by his tie and shook him so hard the manager's eyeglasses flew into the Fryalator. We had to shut it down in order to drain all the oil and we couldn't serve Ringo Fries or Hop Sing Rings the rest of the night.

After a week of double duty I became exhausted and knew I had little future at Bonanza. One morning I arrived to find the manager in the dish area who wasted no time letting me know how disappointed he was in my work and just look around this dish room it was disorganized and the machine was not properly drained the night before. I wasn't working fast enough on the line when we were busy and for the next two weeks he put me on some kind of trial and at the end of the two weeks I would be assessed and he would let me know if I have a job with Bonanza or not. I walked on the spot.

♦♦♦

This is the kind of party I couldn't have worked ten years ago. These medications weren't widely available then. Sales Reps from a pharmaceutical company pitching with a slide show to a room full of mental health care professionals on the merits of a new medication that returns sex drive back to those who've lost it from anti-depressants and anti-anxiety medication. All sorts of questions arise about specific cases and specific medications and the Reps have all the answers with figures and case studies. The dinner is four courses and the bar is open and these psychiatrists and psychologists eat and drink course after course and bottle after bottle of wine and the people who were originally subdued and conservative are now drunk and boisterous waving their hands in the air the noise level in the room has tripled.

They remain late and make long goodbyes. I wonder how early their morning appointments are, and when they finally leave we clean the tables of silverware, glassware, nearly-empty wine bottles, stray dessert plates with half-eaten pieces of Chocolate Cloud Cake. Barb presents the bill to the woman in charge. I hear them negotiating and by the sound of the manager's voice something's not right. The woman is trying to squeeze a last minute discount off the bill with promises to bring future events here because she likes the place very much.

Barb doesn't budge. She books these parties from the very first inquiry through every meeting thereafter and knows some times the struggle continues to the very end, presenting that bill and getting someone to pay. Any small thing goes wrong it could come back to haunt us. And it could be anything. The mirror in the women's room wasn't clean or the children's pasta dishes should have been served before adult meals not with them. The mother-in-law didn't like the main course. The service was slow or they waited too long between courses.

It's always the same with people who are looking to book a banquet. Business functions are generally easier, someone looking to book a bridal shower or a fiftieth anniversary party has more emotional investment than someone looking to make profits from depressed people's sex life. But they want a deal. If they get a quote for forty dollars per person, they want it for thirty-five or they want the forty-five dollar ingredients. They want to know why there has to be so many servers when they'd be the first to complain if their service lacked in any way. Can they bring their own booze and if not why not? Can they come in for dinner on a Saturday night and have the chef cook up some banquet items for them to sample? Can they bring their own cake they ask, only to become outraged when informed of a plating fee.

When the food and beverages are free people eat differently from when they pay for it themselves. The guy who hates to order a second cocktail or glass of wine is slurring his words at the end of a banquet having drunk too many to count. The drunks barely have the last sip down and they are waving for me to get them another. The people who eat light or share an entrée when they dine out are following the servers who carry hors d'oeuvres trays, shoving baby lamb chops, slices of pizetta and grilled shrimp down asking each other with their mouths full when do we get dinner?

◆◆◆

After Bonanza I knew there'd be no going back to the kitchen. The front of the house was my future. George's letter in hand I set out to find a waiter job. I visited all the fancier eateries in the area but this was the 1970s and fine dining had yet to hit the Boston suburbs. There were a number of upscale steak and fish houses so I filled out applications taken by hostesses who promised to pass them along to the manager. I didn't hear back.

One day I stopped at a newer place near the Burlington Mall. I was asked to wait and a few minutes later a manager appeared. He looked me over, read my application and letter, then asked how much waiter experience I had. I stretched it some. He left and a few moments later returned with another manager who looked over my papers asked me the same questions as the first manager and then they left together and returned in five minutes. Someone was leaving and they needed a waiter on the night crew. They'd give me a chance but I'd have to prove myself. I went home with a hundred-plus-page waiter's manual and a job at The Greenhouse in Burlington, Massachusetts. My training would begin the following night.

In all my years as server I have never seen the likes of the waiter's manual and the intensity of the training that I received at The Greenhouse. It was a corporate system, made of a handful of like restaurants, each with its own theme and name such as The Greenhouse whose theme was a greenhouse with its glass roof and plants overflowing everywhere. The Beverly Depot was located in an old train station and the waiters wore engineer outfits. The Public Library, located in Boston, had walls of books on shelves.

Every restaurant was run the same way with the exact same menu and system so that theoretically any waiters, bartenders, cooks or managers could be transplanted from one restaurant to the next. Three regional managers often visited and sat around a dinner table studying their watches to see that the French onion soup came out in less than five minutes or that their steak didn't take longer than the manual allotted, and when their food arrived they'd sit there examining and poking rather than eating. The regional managers looked like different versions of each other. They were short, overweight, pale, beards, eyeglasses, tan pants, penny-loafers, sweater vests, blue shirts with red ties and blue sport coats. Each had a penchant for rapidly scratching their under-chin.

The servers worked in a three-person system. The lead waiter greeted parties, served beverages and took dinner orders. The follow-up waiter remained in the section clearing dinner plates, serving coffee and taking dessert orders. The aid waiter ran food when not watering or breading tables. Everyone overlapped depending on how busy it was and who needed what as the aid sometimes needed help bringing food out or the lead might need someone to take an order.

I poured over the manual that first week memorizing the ingredients of every sauce and each type of steak and how the Boston schrod was baked and what types of booze went into each drink and how to take the order since every table had a number and every seat had a number and I had to take the order according to the number and place it into the kitchen so that the cooks would place the order up according to the numbers and anyone from another section could take an order out and set it down at the correct place. And the drink orders were ordered at the bar in a certain way and the bartender made them in a certain way everything was for efficiency. Rye, gin, rum, vodka, bourbon, scotch. Shot drinks followed by pours, shaken, shaken cream drinks. They were placed on the bar in the order ordered.

It helped that I scored well on the written test my first week. On the floor I grew flustered when it got busy and became overwhelmed. I worked only as an aid in the beginning but it seemed too much work to be doing at once. My trainer kept barking out orders and I couldn't keep them straight in my mind. Bread to table seven, water table fifteen, bread at six and your light's on which meant there was a pick-up in the kitchen. My biggest problem was carrying plates as it was hand service and I had problems stacking plates up my arm.

At the end of the week the two managers took me in the office and basically said they liked me and it was nothing personal but it didn't look as if I could make it. They pointed to my weaknesses while I made much of the fact that I had only worked with trays in the past and I would get the hand service down. Hadn't I scored well on the test? I pleaded with them to give me another week they wouldn't be sorry. They must have figured hiring and training someone else would take more time and I knew from the buzz of the staff they were short-handed so they gave me another chance and I made good. At some time during that next week I suddenly found myself watering, breading and picking up my food without being told. In addition, I was effortlessly carrying heavy plates up my arm, loaded with thick cuts of prime rib, sirloin steaks, surf and turf, baked potatoes and rice pilaf.

For the next four months I worked only as an aid, never getting any drink or dinner orders, never the privilege of greeting a party. Bread, water and deliver appetizers, dinners and desserts from the kitchen. That was it. I received a full cut of tips once I had the aid position down, but the leads and follow-ups had been there much longer than me and preferred not to do the aid position by far the most physically demanding. Eventually I trained as a follow-up, then lead, and within the year I was as efficient at each position as anyone and in time I became one of the trainers at The Greenhouse.

♦♦♦

Last night I had a waiter dream. Or nightmare. It was at the end of a particularly long day, one of the special days like Mother's Day. We're all running around tired and beat at closing time trying to take care of the last diners but the manager is still seating people. I bring a tray full of coffee out from the waiter station to see that I have several new parties and the manager is seating me again. There's no way I can get to all of the parties at once and I ask another waiter aren't we supposed to be closed and he says we're going to stay open until the food is gone and the kitchen is calling food to be picked up and I have desserts to order after-dinner-drinks waiting at the bar new parties looking around because I can't get to them. The manager is taking more names for a waiting list and I start running around telling everyone that we can't do this we will be here all night.

Some of my waiter dreams are serial dreams. At least it seems that way after I wake up. I could swear I've dreamed about that very same restaurant and set of circumstances in the past. In one serial dream I've started working at this posh place with multi-level indoor and outdoor seating. Outside is a lush garden of flowers, green vegetation of every sort, exotic trees and a fountain. I'm wearing black waiter pants and a short white jacket with a white tuxedo shirt and black bow tie, slowly realizing that I have tables in all sections on various levels inside and out. I ask the manager doesn't it make sense to keep a waiter's section in the same general area but he gives me a hostile response so it's not long before I'm running up and down stairs to the kitchen and trying to find my way back to the bar thinking to myself over and over that this can't be done!

◆◆◆

During my tenure at The Greenhouse I was single. Drugs and sex were still above board in the 70s. A waitress and I had a contest to see who could sleep with the most people in one week. My number was hardly impressive for those times but she beat me by three.

I dated a waitress from the night crew, a waitress from the day crew, and a hostess. All of it went largely unnoticed as each was caught up in our own web-weave. Married managers had their pick of the cutest waitresses, and I walked into the wine room to find a cocktail waitress giving one manager a blowjob. A married cashier was having a go with one of the high school bus boys. Waitress and cook affairs were not uncommon. Waitresses and waiters frequently went home with customers they met that night. My line was simple enough, I would be finished with my shift soon would you like to have a drink in the lounge? One of the waiters had slept with every waitress in the place at one time or another. Or should I say they had slept with him.

The drug of choice was cocaine. Not for me as the stuff made me nervous and introverted. Unlike other people who could save the world after a few lines, I found myself sitting in a corner turning my ring around my finger not saying a word. And I saw too quickly how easily it drained one's economy.

I watched the servers and bartenders lose an entire shift's tips for the night's privilege of serving people while high on cocaine. I preferred pot, ubiquitous at the time. Quite often after our employee meal staff members would sneak out the back door and share a joint. If the manager came out he most likely joined in.

The hard partying went on after work beginning with the first shift drink. The shift drink being one allotted by the management when we were counting up our money, continuing until the following morning when I woke to a joint on a sofa with the memory of the previous night chugging past. Drinks at work. Wine and beer later over hours of arguments about politics and God. Acoustic guitar jams followed by phone calls from neighbors to stop the noise. People huddled over the coffee table snorting lines then rubbing their noses. More weed. Cigarettes. English muffins with peanut butter at five o'clock in the morning. Driving home rush hour commuters on their way to work go right to bed.

Fun aside I owe The Greenhouse, there I became a real waiter. I learned how to greet a party. How to get the drink they want when they want it. How to take an order. How to write that order so that cooks could read it and other waiters know exactly who should be getting what and where, including regular and special cooking instructions. I learned how to stand at one table, take an order with seemingly full attention while scanning my section with a corner of one eye to see who needed another drink or dinner plates cleared. I learned how to walk out of the kitchen with a stack of plates while an au jus in an overfull ramekin dripped scalding hot on my arm and knowing there was no going back using power of mind to ignore it while winding my way to the table, placing the plates down and asking pleasantly if anyone needed anything else while my arm skin singed. I learned the art of timing, well placed orders made the entire section operations work as smoothly as possible. I learned about wine service and the various types and varieties of grapes. I learned about the numerous drinks traditional and trendy. I learned to keep a plan in my head constantly aware of my next several moves but ready to be flexible because anything could arise like being on my way to get coffee going for dessert drinks suddenly a man stops me and hands me his overcooked steak which I must bring in the kitchen in an instant my plan is off track meanwhile other tasks are backing up. There are order takers and there are waiters and at The Greenhouse I learned to be a waiter.

On a busy night hundreds and hundreds of people passed through the place. Waiters and waitresses rushed around, bus boys worked up a sweat, managers looked panicked as the wait for a table got longer. Some people refused to wait others accepted and found themselves in an overcrowded lounge no tables or seats open people often returned and stood around the hostess stand alternating looks at their watches and the hostess. Everyone needed help but few were free enough to offer any. Hour after hour I was flat out trying to survive the next crisis and stay afloat in my section.

The menus were simple then. That helped. Steaks, chops, prime rib. Shrimp, scallops, schrod. Or a combination surf and turf. I needed meat cooking instructions and choice of baked potato or rice pilaf. Only other choice the salad dressing and that was later changed when the place installed a salad bar. Most of the cooking was done by prep-people during the day. Line cooks had to grill meat, place pre-portioned fish in the oven, bake the potatoes and cook rice pilaf. It was like a factory.

The tone at The Greenhouse was suburban. All of the clientele came from surrounding suburban towns, as well as the local businesses growing up around Route 128. Nearly all of the staff lived locally, some of them still lived at home. There were a few transplants like a waiter from Morocco. He had a penchant for spitting in people's salads if they gave him a hard time. "Cock suckers" he said then delivered the salads placing them down with a sly grin. We came to call this Moroccan Dressing.

A Canadian hostess spoke with a Canuck accent. But mostly we were American, white and hetero. Typically the hostesses were exceptionally pretty, so were the cocktail waitresses but they seemed or played dumb. The food waitresses were generally cute too. Here you found humanities majors, leftover hippies, newly married area housewives. It was similar with the waiters, many of whom were in college and laid-back hippie types, one or two already married with a day job doing this for some extra cash and the chance to date a hostess or waitress. The cooks were working class guys who preyed on the female employees. Kitchen managers were company men brought in from the home office on the north shore.

So I worked at The Greenhouse for several years, sharpening my skills and digging the party. Eventually I fell in love and moved in with my life-long companion Molly. We wanted to live close to the city, and I was attending the University of Massachusetts in Boston so we found a basement apartment in Cambridge. The commute to Burlington was unnecessary with all of the restaurants around and before I gave notice I spoke with the manager about a transfer to the company's restaurant in Boston. He checked with the home office and it happened they needed someone at

The Public Library so I interviewed with the manager and everything worked out as I'd hoped. Within a few weeks I said goodbye to all of my comrades over the past years, vowed to keep in touch, and made my way to the city.

♦♦♦

Originally a history major in college, most of the books that I read were history related. Then I discovered The Beats. Molly and I had yet to move in together but were often in each other's company. Beyond our mutual interest music, Molly was a reader and a painter. As we spent more time in each other's company our discussions broadened from Patti Smith and David Bowie to literature and art. Browsing her bookshelves I came across a copy of Ginsberg's *Howl*. I read it, astounded, could this be poetry? Soon I came to Kerouac and I have never been the same since. Kerouac's prose cut right into me. Skill-less and unread I made up my mind that I was going to be a writer, no matter what it took.

I switched my major to English and enrolled in introduction to literature courses where I discovered Hawthorne, Thoreau, Whitman, Dickinson, Twain and Kate Chopin. I began reading fervently on my own in no organized way. After devouring the Beat writers I found Henry Miller, Dostoyevsky, Charles Bukowski and poets like e.e. cummings, Kenneth Rexroth and Dylan Thomas. I started writing poems and short stories vowing never to give up even if it meant that I'd grow old and have a shelf full of unpublished books. Molly understood, she wanted to be a painter. We moved into the basement apartment in Cambridge shortly thereafter.

◆◆◆

Sometimes I don't know why we give them menus. They should just say what they want and have the chef cook it. Why should the chef bother working on a dish for weeks, honing each last detail of sauces, vegetables, starches, seasonings, overall flavors and textures to have this woman redo the entire dish? She's allergic to garlic. She wants it done with as little fat as possible. Substitute the tomato pie for plain rice. Is there another vegetable because she hates asparagus? She likes her salmon cooked well done. Ed will love this order. And *Tell the chef to put the sauce on the side* she says and taps her hand on my arm a tap for every stressed word.

I pull my arm away.

When her dinner arrives she waves at me while I'm in the middle of taking another order and I put up my index finger and nod to assure here I will be right there.

She hands me her plate.

This fish is raw. And I wanted plain white rice this is some kind of pilaf.

Oh, I'm sorry madam I'll take this right back for you.

The chef proceeds to burn her already well-done piece of salmon and says that's the closest thing he has to white rice.

She waves me down again.

Where's the dinner?

Should be out any minute. It's Saturday night and the kitchen is very busy.

Well everyone else is now finished here.

In a few moments I return with her charred piece of salmon, explain about the rice and watch her out of the corner of my eye, a puss on her face, probing her food rather than eating it. I clear her table and bring dessert menus. Before anyone else picks up a menu she interrupts me as I am trying to mention the dessert special.

I want the Chocolate Cloud Cake without the raspberry sauce and whipped cream on the side.

I guess she's no longer fat conscious. As I am clearing plates from a nearby table she waves me down again. This time I pretend I didn't see and walk right past into the waiter station where I take a sip on a cup of coffee with Irish Cream then slip out the back into the kitchen where I pick up food to deliver. Next time she sees me she waves her napkin.

I ordered a tea.

Yes madam it's steeping as we speak.

Still?

Yes.

Well I don't want mine too strong.

During the entire dinner the other three people in her party pay no mind. They continue on with their conversation without interruption as if this happens all the time and they're conditioned to it. She sends the tea back it's too strong demands that I bring the tea and hot water so she can steep the tea herself. It's times like this one considers a dash of Moroccan dressing. The tip is fourteen percent but more of an insult on the way out the woman complains to the hostess that the food wasn't very good and she doesn't know what's wrong with the waiter but he can't seem to get anything right and every time she needed me I was nowhere to be found.

♦♦♦

The Public Library menu had higher prices then The Greenhouse and the sophisticated clientele tended to tip better. I automatically made more money and diners were slightly less demanding. The greater part of the wait staff consisted of gay men. There were a few women, one of whom was a lesbian and an actress. Besides myself there was one other straight man on the floor. The floor manager made it all very clear when I interviewed and asked if that would be any problem for me working with gay men. It wouldn't and it never was.

Unlike the white suburban crew in the kitchen at The Greenhouse, the cooking at The Public Library was done by young Latinos, blacks from the inner city and newly migrated Haitians who rose to the task on those busy week-end nights putting out hundreds of steaks and chops to order, prime rib, chicken, fish and shrimp. During my tenure the biggest problem at The Public Library was finding and keeping dishwashers. It was a revolving door of borderline street people, stoner high school kids, guys just out of prison, illegal aliens and cousins of illegal aliens.

The wait staff was also older than that at The Greenhouse. Many of the waitrons, as they were called to maintain a sense of androgyny, were college graduates or in graduate school. Few were interested in finding what was referred to as a straight job. They were carefree, content to work as waiters and go out to the bars after hours to look for sex, party and have days free for going to the beach, the gym, and dining out on nights off. They loved to have fun, were cynics and obsessed with sex. I quickly got used to their waiter station talk, not much different from the banter of waiters at The Greenhouse about a woman we found attractive at a table.

Did you see him at fifty-two?
Mmmhmm.
Doesn't he know?
Not yet.

Well, better latent than never.

I learned that *doesn't he know* referred to a man who they believed was gay but was still living straight. The consensus seemed to be that most men were homosexual and either latent or simply didn't have a clue yet. It was the reverse of straight men believing gay men choose to be gay or there's simply something wrong with them that needs to be fixed. But the fact that I could be raunchy and cynical as the *girls,* as they liked to call themselves, played well and they accepted me.

The gay men were usually impeccable about their appearance and grooming. There were several amongst the crew, one of whom called himself Princess Daisy, who finished their faces with a little make-up. They had their hair cut by the best cutters around town and were as quick to criticize a woman's appearance as another man's.

Did you see that face on table thirty-three?

How could I not?

She looks like she put her make-up on with a spatula.

I know.

Worrying when they had to add one inch to their waistlines, they made me so self-conscious I found myself checking my ass in the dressing room mirror as one of them asked passive-aggressively had I gained some weight.

No, uh, I don't think so does it look it?

Maybe. It shows a little on your face.

And then there was Chub. Chub was the other straight guy on the floor. He lived his entire life in nearby Charlestown and was overweight and bald in his late twenties. He wasn't much on grooming and his uniforms were often wrinkled and in need of laundering. Chub had a love/hate relationship with the other waiters. He verbally held them in contempt because of their sexual preference, but it was clear that he liked them despite calling them Baloney Pony Jockeys or Sword Swallowers.

◆◆◆

I've never recovered from the changeover to a computer system at Tulips. After all these years, despite my own mistakes and imperfections, hand-written dupes were all I knew. I've written thousands of food and drink orders, special instructions scribbled in and around the edges, table numbers and seat numbers, first course and second course, adding each check with a calculator. Most of that wouldn't change, I was told. Take the order the same old way but transfer the information into the computer. I no longer walk to the kitchen and drop off my food order, or go to the bar and drop off my drink order. Now I press the buttons and my food order pops up in the kitchen and drink order at the bar. When finished waiting on the party I press a button and the computer adds the check and prints out a perfect receipt.

But I can't catch on. I make mistakes and plenty of them. I often find myself pressing the wrong button so that I order an extra dinner or appetizer, or forget to order something or add special instructions or get tables crossed so that people are bringing my food to the wrong tables no matter how hard I concentrate when I am at the computer the worse it gets. I continually call the manager to correct errors with her master key. Everyone else on the staff seems to have no problem and remarks how the system's making it easier. I can't figure out how to time things when I need to fire a second course there's always someone using the computers so the course gets fired late or I forget to fire it. These things refuse to become second nature—as if somehow my server memory can't take on one more crumb of information after all these years.

I run around like a rookie. In the morning my legs ache. It used to be only after an extremely busy Saturday night I'd notice a bit of soreness. Now I work a slow Tuesday, make mistakes and run around for short money then hurt on Wednesday morning. To work a Saturday and make the big money means getting beat up. I return home with two nights' pay but I am physically useless for a day and a half later. There seems no middle ground. Some evenings I work the bar. If folks eat dinner at the bar I make out but even there I mess up on the computer. I hit the soup for salad key or put wrong course numbers. Sometimes I stare confused at the screen until I strike any button out of panic while the bar customers wait for me to have a free moment so that they can talk to me about sports, wine, food, and how long the restaurant's been open.

◆◆◆

Chub was one of the crudest people I ever knew. At first I couldn't imagine how the management let him out on the floor to serve food. Soon I learned that what he lacked in physical appearance he made up for with his physical strength. It was clear that while others had finesse, Chub was simply the strongest waiter on the floor in more ways than one. He could do more than anyone, whether it be carrying huge cocktail trays overloaded with drinks, stacking dishes up his arm, or clearing plates from a table Chub maintained a sense of the room like no one else. He knew what was happening at any given time and what needed to be done before it needed to be done. It was marvelous to see him barreling through the kitchen door into the dining room, beads of sweat on his balding forehead, his left arm laden down with heavy plates bursting with fat pieces of rare prime rib, baked potatoes and hot au jus in glass cups some of the hot juices spilling onto his arm Chub never once flinching.

Eventually I found that he had a softer side, especially when dealing with customers he could be quite gentle. Chub helped me out during those early days at The Public Library. Soon he began to call me The Dago and I didn't mind. We came from working class backgrounds, grew up in the Boston area and shared street lore. Moreover, the fact that I was straight gave him a new ally. Chub would pull me aside, give me some pointers on how to buffalo the floor manager because there were things the floor manager paid particular attention to like making sure chairs were very clean at set-up or when he's nearby let him see you wiping out glasses and sure enough the floor manager began remarking how pleased he was with me and I found myself with a good schedule which meant Friday and/or Saturday night and nights off earlier in the week.

Chub and I also shared a liking for weed. It wasn't long before we established a ritual of smoking after the staff meal before we opened. We'd take a walk across the terrace or maybe drive around the block in Chub's old Buick Riviera. I never worried about management when I was with Chub. He certainly didn't and I got the feeling Chub basically did whatever he wanted. If I asked what-if, he simply waved my worry off. I remember a young kitchen manager arguing with Chub until the manager threw Chub out of the kitchen. Chub reached across the cook-line, grabbed the guy by his throat and lifted him up on his toes. It was the kind of thing a waiter would surely get fired for but the next night Chub was working on the floor and the kitchen manager grilling with an imprint of Chub's hand on his throat.

I found the gay men's personalities ran from the most stereotypical queens to men who seemed to be straight. But no mistake about it sex was the constant topic every night. Who got it when and where, which one was covered with cum, were frequent staff dinner conversations. The queens had nicknames like Princess Daisy and Bobby Jo. One of the hot places for cruising late at night was the nearby Fens where Princess Daisy once did thirteen men. He called it his Baker's Dozen. There was an obnoxious young son-of-a-factory owner who was so white he looked as if he could be an albino and he had a liking for fucking very black men. A guy named Jimmy, a carpenter by trade, had to pass for straight at his day job. They had their own way of saying things like nice to she you or how are you girly.

Some nights after work, I went to the bars. There were bars where young boys hung out and bars where old men went and bars where you might see guys having sex in the corner and I spied a man giving himself a blowjob and an S & M bar where men in leather could be heard swapping brownie recipes and some walked each other around on leashes. The guys from work were always teasing me about going over to their church. This was all before AIDS and it would be a year or two later when I remember a few of the waiters having a conversation about the disease each asking the others what they knew or heard. Some of those waitrons would be early casualties.

During those initial years at The Public Library I honed my skills, became more familiar with wine and with the urban clientele became a polished, professional waiter. I earned good money. Weeknights were steady but never busy to the point of chaos. Weekends the restaurant ran a one or two hour wait for a table. We turned our sections at least three times sometimes even a partial fourth. The menu was simplified, the system close to perfect, and the waitrons I worked with were some of the finest I would ever know. Nights I worked with Chub, no matter our third partner, we ran like a machine and made the most tips at the end of the night. It wasn't finesse service, but endurance. By the time the section filled up around quarter to seven, you knew it was going to be head down no stopping until midnight. Meat and potatoes. Stuffed shrimp and rice. Wine out of jugs.

♦♦♦

I'm always bemused at the way they react when they find out I'm a writer. It shouldn't come as any surprise. There are probably more artists in the restaurant business, pound for pound, than any other industry. I've worked with jazz, rock, folk and classical musicians—sculptors, dancers, female impersonators, actors, singers, photographers, poets and novelists—I even worked with a guy who painted with spoons. I guess they want to know what I do with my time during the day. Is this my second job? Why else, they must wonder, would someone my age be doing this?

I tell them I'm a writer. They act impressed. I know the next question. Yes I am published. Might they have heard me?

Probably not.

What are the names of your books?

I tell them. They look puzzled. If I publish novels what am I doing here? I attempt an abridged account of the publishing industry. They're bewildered. Then a friendly grin, perhaps they figured it out—I can't be much of a writer if

I publish books and tend bar for a living. The regulars are more annoying.

How's the writing going?

When are we going to read the best seller?

Still working on the great American novel?

Still writing?

Are you writing these days?

Do they think after five, ten or twenty years I'm going to stop writing? Do I ask are you still a dentist, insurance broker, lawyer? They haven't read any of my books so how do they know I haven't already written the great American novel? What is the great American novel, anyhow? They try to lend support, assure me I'll write that best seller yet and make it to the big time. I refill their drinks and empty ashtrays.

There are ones who ask do I know a certain book. If I haven't heard of it they look perplexed. How could a writer not have heard of the one book they've read in the last five years? Worse, the next time they come in they bring a copy of the book to lend me. Very next time they want to know did I read the book. Eventually I read a book I don't want to read so I can discuss it the following week and get it over with. Sometimes they ask how they can find my books I tell them online. They try to remain enthused. I give them the names of the books and sites where they can be found. They never mention the books again. They're not in bookstores she asks.

Now and again they bring their own. Poetry. Predictable rhymes. Sing-song meter or worse, rhymes at the end of free verse lines. Love. Ocean walks. Sunrises. Deep thoughts. Stories, or parts of stories never finished. More love. Oceans. Deep thoughts. Personal traumas. They too had notions of creativity, of the life of the artiste, as they are fond to call it.

But something came up along the way. Marriage. Financial pressure. Lack of time. Someday they intend to return to it.

Poems and stories are typed, others handwritten. Nonetheless they expect a response. Right then and there. They'll hand me a poem, expect me to read it as they explain circumstances surrounding it, and what it means. When I've read it they wait like dogs for a biscuit, as if with a wave of my hand I'll confirm something they need to hear. I pour beers, shake cocktails, cash out checks and serve bar food. I tell them very nice. Very nice indeed.

My daughter wants be a writer.

Twenty thousand a year for college. I told her it wouldn't put any bread on the table.

You should write a book about this business.

It's been done.

Oh, yes, what was the name of that book?

I think it was a best seller.

I can't remember.

♦♦♦

Eventually a position on the bar opened. Chub had bartending experience and got the job. He became a great bartender though you wouldn't think so to see his bulging body behind the bar. No one could do more at once than Chub. He'd be drawing draft beers, shaking and mixing drinks, pouring wine behind his back. In time he developed a good relationship with the bar regulars, the ones who came in four, five, or seven nights a week. The service tips from the wait staff and the tips from diners having a drink before dinner were one thing—but you made real money from the regulars.

The bar manager left for a straight job, Chub asked for

and got the manager position. He asked me if I wanted to come over to the bar. It would mean more money and the shifts were longer but I could work fewer of them. I was just beginning graduate school at the time and it seemed like it could work for me. I had never tended bar but had an understanding of ingredients and making drinks. Chub assured me he'd teach me what I needed to know. We worked several training shifts together then I was on my own. I slid into the work with no problems.

The mahogany bar was long and shiny. Fifteen tall stools stood in front of it. The cocktail lounge consisted of twenty wooden tables and fifty or so chairs. The lounge clientele were professionals, medical people from nearby hospitals— or daters sitting in the quiet, dimly lit corners. Bar clientele consisted of mostly regulars.

I worked Saturday, Sunday and Monday nights. On Saturday nights there were two of us. Sunday and Monday I worked alone. When busy I could easily sink in the weeds. A bunch of regulars were demanding enough, and if the dining room and cocktail lounge were busy there was too much to do and not enough time or hands to do it. I made more money than I ever made as a server. I learned from Chub you could get away with a lot more untaxed cash than working as a waiter. If a regular threw you a twenty dollar bill, if ten regulars threw you a twenty, who knew?

Cab never missed a night—often twice per night. They called him Cab because he drove a cab. I don't know why they didn't call him Taxi. Cab was down to earth, had a thousand stories and a great sense of humor. Everyone loved him. Twice divorced he had a couple of sons and liked to take them fishing. Cab loved to fish. He also loved beer. Cab drove seven days a week. Mornings, afternoons and evenings, depending on his hangover on any given day. He said no matter how much he made he never had enough for child support and his own expenses. Cab often appeared first. No sooner did I open the door he's parking his cab out front. I'd give him a longneck and light his cigarette.

What's new?

Not much. You?

Same old.

What could possibly be new since I said goodnight after last night's closing? I'd ask him how's business. Barely enough to make cab rent. One more beer before he hits the pavement. I'd light another cigarette for him. Melanie the cocktail waitress walked past, Cab looked at me, blew smoke out his mouth and shook his head.

Man she is something else.

Mike arrived and before he even sat down ordered himself a gin and tonic and another beer for Cab. Cab said that he had to hit the road but Mike insisted. This meant that Cab had to buy one back for Mike so Cab was actually here for two more not one. A few people trickled in and out of the lounge. I made some drinks for waitrons serving in the dining room. By the time Mike and Cab drank their two drinks, Dick was walking through the lounge even though he should have been working next door at the theater. Cab said that he was getting out of here before he got in trouble. He closed his check and on the way out Dick tried to get him to return for one more but this time Cab was firm and left for work.

Mike, the self-proclaimed regular of the year, year after year, was over six feet, a former high school basketball star. He claimed to know more about sports than anyone. At home he had a shrine to Larry Bird in his living room and boasted the biggest sports library around. Mike was a Navy

veteran and when he got into arguments he was fond of saying that he was in the Navy, traveled around the world and
seen a lot things. Mike managed a warehouse said he made
good money and spent it like he did.

Mike loved buying drinks for others. Run the shoe we
called it, a round for everyone. I never knew what it came
from. Run the shoe. I don't know where 86-it came from. But
it meant there is none of an item left and woe to the server
who ordered a dish that was 86'd. Working the wood—bartending. Bars have traditionally been wood. Working the
stick came from the beer tap handles. Mike would tell me
to run the shoe, build up big checks and leave excessive
tips. His wife would phone they'd argue. Other times Mike
would want me to tell her that he wasn't there but I wouldn't.
Occasionally Mike brought his wife in with him. They'd
meet after work. After a few drinks they would either argue
or be all over each other.

Dick bought Mike a round and Mike bought Dick
a round. They talked about baseball. Dick managed the
theater next to the restaurant. Dick was on doctor's orders
not to drink or smoke. A year previous he went through triple
bypass surgery. Dick was always dressed gentlemanly, with a
jacket and tie and shined shoes and his red hair brushed back.
He loathed his wife and called her She-Who-Must-Be-Toler-
ated. They had two teenage children together. Dick told Mike
his Ted Williams story. Dick told his Ted Williams story at
least once a night when the opportunity arose. He'd always
been sickly. Even as a kid. And somehow his childhood hero
visited him in the hospital. Newspaper people took photos.
Dick said that was the greatest day of his life, a great man Ted
Williams coming to visit him in the hospital, and Dick blew
smoke out his mouth.

Timmy always arrived late. He had a hard time getting started in the morning so he scheduled his appointments from mid-morning until mid-evening. The only one of the group who graduated from college, Timmy earned a living as a psychotherapist. During his absence some of the guys joked what a scary concept Timmy giving council. Timmy was quiet and when he drank a lot his eyes blazed red. He wore slightly long hair and a beard, sweaters and wool blazers. Timmy usually rubbed his beard when he first arrived as if deep in contemplation. He'd drink soda water with lemon after that beer and scotch. Timmy was fond of boats and the ocean. He owned a Boston Whaler and on weekend afternoons he would take the guys out and they'd end up at the bar drunk full of stories from the day's adventure in Boston Harbor.

The shift began at three-thirty. We did most of the bar stocking at the end of the shift so setting up involved wiping down bar and stools, putting out bottles of booze, filling the bins up with ice, cutting fruit, filling juice containers, checking for Bloody Mary mix, sour mix, Margarita mix, stocking bar napkins, candles, straws. We opened at four-thirty and generally folks were waiting at the door to get in. Last call was at twelve-twenty. By the time we cleaned up and people left it was one or later. There were no breaks. I stood on my feet from three-thirty to one. Some time before the kitchen closed they sent me out dinner. I ate bites of it in-between making drinks.

♦♦♦

Molly and I married around the time I finished my B.A. in English. It seemed like the right thing to do, two huge transitions at the same time. The restaurant business had been a great way to support myself in college. My schooling finished, I faced a new dilemma: where do I go from here? Writing was still my passion and staying in the food business would be a fine way to support myself. At the same time I felt as if I wanted more, I thought there was more to do in the way of schooling so I enrolled in a graduate program in English at U. Mass. Boston. Eventually I could teach and write, instead of being a server and writer. I remember expressing this idea to a teacher at the university. She laughed in my face. You and everyone else was her response. Nonetheless I pressed on.

My poems and stories had come a long way in the course of several years, but I still wrote imitations of the writers who mattered to me. Graduate school was intense and I loved the reading and being around people who were passionate about literature. I also enrolled in graduate writing courses and found students more talented than I. I studied Joyce, Whitman, Modernism and the history of criticism. I took a course called Studies in Poetry and learned about meter, rhyme schemes, sonnets, villanelles and haiku while reading Sappho to poets of the twentieth century. Somewhere around this time I began my first novel, an autobiographic tale about my relationship with Molly and my experiences working the bar at The Public Library. The characters seemed handed to me on a platter. Often I woke up in the morning and wrote about what occurred and what I overheard the night before at the bar.

I began sending my poems out at this time. Clueless about the realities of publication, I purchased a guide to literary magazines and sent out packets of poems to magazines I'd never set my eyes upon as well as major publications like *The New Yorker* and *Poetry*. The form rejection letters came back as fast as I could put postage on my manuscripts. Publication seemed essential to me during those days, desperate for the acceptance and the notoriety that I assumed certain to follow. The rejection hurt, but didn't discourage me. It seemed the more negative response I received the more I wrote.

♦♦♦

Betty Ann and Ed met at a restaurant where they worked. She served food and Ed worked in the kitchen. Eventually they married and not long afterwards opened Tulips. By that time Ed had perfected his skills as a chef at several area restaurants. Tulips had been a risky investment. Located in Arlington—next to Cambridge—it was thought that most suburban people preferred to dine in the city, likely to drive past a place in their own town. Nevertheless for Ed and Betty Ann, it meant an affordable lease and an opportunity not to stand toe-to-toe with the inner city competition.

Their instincts were right. Arlington had never seen a place like Tulips but Arlington was changing. Soon the word got out that a fine dining establishment had opened where the old savings bank used to be. My tenure began a few months after they'd opened. Instantly I found the crew, Ed and Betty Ann, more pleasurable than any I'd had the pleasure to work with.

Ed and Betty Ann worked seven days a week. Betty Ann managed the office by day, hosted by night and made out the server schedule as our floor manager. She had enormous energy, though she was easily confused. We could set a table for a private party four different ways because she would change her mind each time we set it. We would have to break down a table set for twenty and begin again. Ed was a friendly chef, not too much tension like there can be between cooks and wait staff. Like anyone under pressure he could crack and might leave the cook line to find me in the dining room and yell about a mistake in an order. He had a way of putting up his dishes by specific dish. All the steaks on the board, then all the fish, then all the duck—this meant sometimes items were put up too late, some to early. We learned to live with it.

From a server's point of view Tulips was an ideal set-up. I had a regular schedule posted a month in advance, with a reasonable amount of side-work before and after shifts. Because of its suburban location people tended not to stay as late as in the city. The place was small enough so that three servers could work the room at any time. One bartender worked a small bar and we served only beer and wine. On weeknights with moderate business we made out well. On Friday and Saturday nights the three of us turned the room three times and walked away with our pockets lined.

♦♦♦

By the time I'd shifted to the bar at The Public Library a newer group of waiters made up the server staff. The older gay men were leaving, replaced by younger straight folks— new-wavers of sorts, finishing college or working their way through graduate school. The kitchen changed too when the crew was replaced after a theft of steaks and booze. Gravy, the new kitchen manager, had long unkempt hair, a beard and beer belly. He worked in the company's kitchens for years but he wasn't really a company man. He always kept an open bottle of beer in the refrigerator next to the cook line.

Gravy and Chub bonded immediately. They liked to think of themselves as Men's Men. Each of them loved sports, gambling, and drinking. On his off nights Chub would come to the bar and at the end of his shift Gravy would sit doing his paper work getting the betting lines on the games. They were always up to something. Making bets or moving weed.

Someone would yell run the shoe and I'd be putting them up and then Cab would call out for shooters so I'd mix up a round. Shooters were anything I might desire to put into the shaker glass as long as it was mostly hard stuff and a bit of juice. I shook the mixture and poured it into small cordial glasses in front of each man. They shot them down in unison.

Thursday began the weekend for the weekend regulars. Friday and Saturday were big nights, and sometimes Sunday for hair of the dog. Weekend regulars knew the six night a week regulars and when the bar was full there'd be twenty guys drinking, smoking, talking sports, women. Drinks were backed up. One guy after another had me run the shoe. Then someone shouted for shooters and I'd mix a batch. As the night wore on and it grew closer to last call, it became more intense. By last call they ordered heavy, put one for yourself on there.

I preferred to smoke. Once the final customers were gone and we locked the door, someone lit up a joint and I'd count out the cash draw, stock, and slip somebody another beer. Gravy rolled joints so big one of them would have kept Woodstock going another day. He took out his bag and put several large buds on the bar. He performed a mock-roll to warm up his fingers. Then instead of filling the paper with grass, rolling it up and licking—he licked the glue side first, connected the two sides to make an empty tube and with a match stick he packed tiny pieces of buds into the paper tube. The joint was so fat and packed it went around for an hour.

Cocaine was everywhere then. I avoided it. I knew some

of the regulars disappeared into the men's room. A few of the new waiters were buzzing around, having private meetings in the waiter station and disappearing into the bathroom. Occasionally one of the regulars might ask if I wanted to do a line, but I declined. Gravy and the general manager regularly disappeared into the manager's office at odd times and the office door was locked. Gravy liked beer, weed, cocaine, gambling, or a combination of any.

Gravy also liked women. But they were slightly lower on his priorities list. Fact is Gravy almost always had a nice woman who was interested in him—sometimes more than one at once. Gravy didn't have a driver's license so he didn't own a car. He would use theirs. He would sleep at their apartments because he lived down on the south shore and he invariably got so drunk he couldn't make the last train out of North Station. The worst Gravy treated his girlfriends the more they seemed to want him. Gravy told every woman he began to see that he didn't want a serious relationship. He was free to do as he pleased. If Chub suddenly came up with tickets to the game, Gravy went even if he had a date. He lived in a house with a bunch of people and bragged that he could fit everything he owned—a few changes of clothes, his pot scale and his *Book of the Tao*, in a duffel bag, and be gone.

Gravy had sold pot for as long as he could remember. During the seventies he smuggled cocaine from Colombia. Gravy bought weed by the pound from Chub. Chub had connections everywhere. Gravy broke the pounds up for sale. Waiters, cooks, corporate managers, friends were his frequent customers. On a day a new shipment arrived there was a line outside of Gravy's kitchen office. Once, Gravy tried to introduce the concept of thirds. Pot was traditionally broken up in fourths. You bought a full ounce, a half an ounce, or a quarter of an ounce. Gravy proposed that you buy an ounce, two-thirds of an ounce, or one-third of an ounce. You'd pay more, but get more. It didn't go over. At one time he put a new pack of rolling papers in the bags he sold. The summer of the endless drought, Gravy contacted a friend in his home-town Cleveland. A few days later the friend phoned from the road, on his way with his trunk full of weed.

Eventually the general manager left and Chub got the position. There would be no bar manager, we worked a set schedule and the other bartenders and I knew our job. In no time Chub had the manager thing down and bought some new suits for his nights working the door. One thing had changed—Chub began to act unfairly towards the waiters—his tone and stance towards them was one of supe-riority. When it was busy and Chub was working the front of the house, he could be a gentleman towards customers and in the waiter station be cussing someone out.

♦♦♦

I gave Tulips one month's notice. There's three weeks left. Three shifts per week makes nine shifts. I could give some or all of them away. Waiters and bartenders are eager for extra work. I'm tired by nine o'clock. I make more mistakes than ever. I become flustered easier. No matter how hard it could be in the past I enjoyed an element of freedom that I found in the work. These past months I've felt chained and approach-ing fifty thinking I've wasted too many years.

Knowing my days are numbered brings an enormous re-lief. So much so I question myself, am I doing the right thing, what will I do for work and how will I make as much money? Suddenly the bar regulars who annoy me don't. The waiters

I don't like are nice people. Ed chases me down about a mistake in an order and I get a kick out of it. I graciously tend to the needs of the most bothersome customers. I don't look at the amount of a tip anyone leaves. What does a fifty-year-old man with no experience at anything but writing and twenty-five years as a server do?

You'll write that best seller yet.

How's the great American novel coming?

How's the writing going?

Do you write every day?

Yes I get up every morning seven days a week, sit down and write as the muse flows mellifluously on the breeze wafting through my open window. Then I shave, take a shower and come here. I would like to serve every day but I'm too tired from all the writing. They discover that I am leaving, wish me luck, assure me when I hit the big time they'll say I knew him when. They ask for another round, can they look at the menu, what are the specials tonight?

The first time I left the business "for good" I worked as a substitute teacher while applying for post-graduate programs. I'd been in the business for about ten years. My goal was to be accepted at a grad school and live on a stipend while working on my Ph.D. I put every hope I had into the plan. I had no alternative. I didn't get in. It was the nadir in my life up to that time. Tired of breaking up fights at the city high school for forty-five dollars a day, I went back to The Public Library. Chub was eager to have me and in one or two shifts it felt as if I never left.

The second time I quit the business I worked as a laborer for a contractor. I dug holes and filled holes. I unloaded lumber and sheet rock. I took a sledgehammer to walls. I carried dusty wreckage and loaded it into dumpsters. Work began at seven in the morning. Coffee break came at ten and we took an hour for lunch at noon then another break about two-thirty while in-between, sheer drudgery. We knocked off at four. During heat waves the day moved in slow motion as sweat flowed and my upper body got deep brown-red. I was paid by the hour, cash under the table. It wasn't so bad a wage, though not what I could make in the business. In the end the hours and lack of mental stimulation got to me. The guys talked about sports, stupid views on politics, women, and their racial prejudices. In the business the people I worked with came from varied backgrounds. They grew up in places around the country, or other countries. There were artists and students. Conversations in the waiter station were stimulating, sometimes hilariously witty, and I felt connected there. So I left the construction business and once again put on the apron.

Two years ago I left Tulips to take some time off, be a house dad at home and figure out what I might want to do in the future. I'd been at Tulips for five years and developed work relationships with most of the people there. Some of them became friends. Barb was a photographer, Marissa a florist, Tiger a Buddhist who practiced Tai Chi, and Lou. Because of the similarity in our ages and interests, we occasionally met for lunch, or dinner and drinks on the Monday nights that Tulips closed. We also had a rock and roll band, Ed, Marissa, myself, a cook and another waiter. We'd practice once in a while and play out. When I left they held a farewell gathering for me after work. Knowing my passion for Italian red wines they presented me with a case of Amarone, one of my favorites. I felt sure this time was going to be the last. There had to be some way I could make money out there without working as a servant. I scanned the papers. I thought about copy editing, technical writing, going back to school to get certified to teach high school English.

Without the extra cash coming in, household funds drained quickly. After six months I phoned Betty Ann to ask if I could be placed on the on-call list. Soon I began picking up an occasional waiter or bar shift and when a waiter gave notice I was given three nights a week. I bit the bullet, but slipped back into the groove seamlessly. The money got better and better at Tulips as business kept increasing. Betty Ann and Ed were doing so well there was talk of expanding. I liked it the way it was, small and casual, no pretense. Expansion would bring white table clothes, dressier uniforms, fancier dishes and glassware, customers with attitude.

♦♦♦

As the eighties wound down, the demand for steak houses declined. This came partly from the prevailing notion that too much red meat was bad for you. But the taste of American diners had changed. There were several Boston chefs making a name. Nouvelle cuisine left a mark. People suddenly wanted more than surf and turf with a glass of jug burgundy. Fine wines arrived from as far away as Australia and New Zealand. Suburbs were slower to feel the effects, in the city The Public Library's business was gradually declining. Word was that the corporation was looking to get out.

Chub surprised me when he said he was trying to purchase the place. Chub always seemed to be doing something off level so I figured he might have a few extra bucks—but not the kind of money to buy The Public Library. Chub went ahead with the negotiations and took on a partner, an old Charlestown buddy named Danny Sullivan who already owned part of a restaurant in New Hampshire but knew nothing about the restaurant business. Weeks became months as parley continued. One week it looked like it was a sure thing. The next week the entire deal was coming apart. Then one day Chub and Danny arrived after a meeting and said they had the deal done and would soon be owners of The Public Library.

Never the same after he owned the restaurant, Chub's drinking increased and he became more of a brute dealing with the staff. He took on a girlfriend. Chub had married a hometown girl two or three years after we met and she was expecting their first child when Chub began fooling around with Erica. Erica was a plain-looking young woman, small and heavy who acted like she was thirteen. Nothing outstanding to commend her to guys her own age—but to Chub, never a looker, she was a princess.

Chub met Erica secretly for lunch. They went to her apartment for sex. At the end of the shift she sat down with Chub for dinner and the staff waited on them. After dinner she followed Chub out to the cocktail lounge where the regulars gathered to watch the game she rubbed Chub's back as they swapped little kisses. Then one night while Chub and Erica where eating dinner, Chub's wife Anne appeared with their six-month-old baby in her arms. She called each of them every name that they could be called then knocked the cocktail and water glasses all over them. Chub moved out of his house for about six months and then his wife let him back.

The face of The Public Library transformed. The professionals were going to the many new and upscale restaurants that were opening around town. They were replaced by tradesmen and working people from nearby Charlestown, Roslindale and Hyde Park. There where several questionable men who came in once or twice a week for dinner. Chub referred to them as VIPs and we treated them thus. One man in particular died his hair red and wore sunglasses and usually had a woman at least half his age on his arm. Another guy was short and homely, balding and overweight. He seemed to have no neck and wore a Boston Celtics jacket. He came in with a guy about sixty, also bald with a red, booze-blossom nose. Chub often sat down with these men, and frequently they disappeared into the office.

Things were changing in the lounge. When Chub took over he immediately installed a wide-screen television. There had never been a television in the bar before. Many of the after work hospital people stopped coming as more of Chub and Danny's friends turned out and the bar could be two deep with drunks cheering on the Celtics or Red Sox. There were some complaints, but Chub didn't care. Within a matter of months the lounge became a sports bar. Any couple looking to have an intimate conversation had to go elsewhere. Local professionals wishing to unwind after work followed suit.

I made more money than ever. The work was hard and the regulars were demanding. They left sizeable tips and expected to be treated accordingly. They ate burgers, wings, steaks, and sandwiches and it was nothing for any of them to consume a dozen drinks per evening. Chub had a policy which was give them one early on the house so they remember, and if they stay give them another free one late. In between it was nothing for Chub to twirl his hand in the air and set them up for everyone and I'd be opening beers like a machine, shaking and mixing drinks. After work if the mood was right the waiters gathered at the bar and Chub opened it up. Music blared from the stereo and waiters and waitresses danced on the bar. I'd mix up a huge batch of shooters and one by one folks would lay their heads over the bar open wide and I would walk down the bar and pour shooters in their mouths.

♦♦♦

I can't imagine how much food I have tossed or seen thrown away. Steak, pork, chicken, duck, rabbit, venison, veal, pâté, shrimp, calamari, clams, lobster, salmon, haddock, grouper, sturgeon, crab cakes, cod, sardines, bluefish, skate, tuna, salads, various green and root vegetables, pasta and mashed potatoes, risottos, soups, appetizers, ice cream, cakes, cookies, pies, chocolate bread pudding, raspberry torte, cheesecake, bread, wine, soda, coffee and tea, butter, bottled water.

I hear somewhere there is an organization that is trying to get this food to people who are hungry. I take a fork and slide everything into the trash then place the plates on the dishwasher line. Night after night I dump half a meal, a quarter of a meal, sometimes an entire meal—table after table. If there's a mistake, perhaps an overcooked steak comes back or a waiter orders wrong, no matter. If it is busy, the chef simply dumps the meal in the trash and tosses the plate out of the way.

As a college student I kept food to eat. Most of us did. It was easy to grab an uneaten pork chop a piece of chicken or cut the eaten end off a piece of prime rib and take the rest home. At the end of the night we could take baked potatoes and rice. I did much of my eating out of the restaurant. Those of us who had pets brought doggy bags home too. At one time I had a beagle and fed him from the restaurant.

Customers can be sticklers about their leftovers, going so far as to request leftover bread. These people have every thing ready when I arrive at the table, their arms wrapped around their bounty. Saying they want all this wrapped using their index finger as if drawing a wide circle around their claim. Others ask for a doggy bag and forget it. Then there are those forced into taking a doggy bag by someone at their table.

Oh, go ahead, don't leave all that.

I don't want it.

You can have it for lunch tomorrow.

No I won't.

Then I'll have it for lunch.

Go ahead.

Well, it's a shame to waste it.

Could you wrap that?

And the bread too?

♦♦♦

I worked my way through graduate school at The Public Library. My three bar shifts per week allowed time for my studies. I received my M.A. in English and found myself in a quandary similar to the one I faced when I finished my B.A. degree. The restaurant business remained a way of supporting my writing with lots of free time in which I could do as I pleased. I still found the business easy and fun so I decided to continue with my writing. I had nearly completed the draft of my first novel—now I could work full time on the revision, and write new poetry as it came.

Outside the confines of the university I could read authors I chose, many of whom the academy ignored. I spent months with Ezra Pound's *Cantos*, Charles Olson's *Maximus Poems*, Louis Zukofsky's *A*, and Gertrud Stein's *The Making of*

Americans. These writers convinced me that the boundaries of literature went beyond what I had been taught in college. My artistic vision expanded.

Around this time I had my first poem accepted for publication in a little magazine called *Wind.* My poem was titled "Ice Out," a cross between Kenneth Rexroth and Robert Creeley. *Wind* was a conventional magazine, with a reputation for taking on new writers, but an established publication nonetheless. The day the acceptance letter arrived Molly and I went out for dinner to celebrate. In all the years and publications since, I don't think I've felt more euphoric. Finally, I was a published writer. The thrill didn't last long. During the following weeks I experienced a tremendous letdown since I had imagined things would somehow change when I became published. My life went on, the people who congratulated me forgot, and my routine returned to business as usual. There was little room in the world for another published poet.

Over the years I'd been attending poetry readings around town and at school. Poets who read were established and conventional—products of the MFA and University Press milieu. It wasn't that the poetry was so bad but most of it didn't ignite anything inside of me. Where were the poets for whom Kerouac, Olson, Stein, Creeley, Williams and others mattered?

One Sunday afternoon I found myself in the basement bar of a restaurant in Cambridge. The reading series was called Word of Mouth and for the first time I felt among writers with whom I had something in common. The type of writing the series supported was closer to writers I was interested in than anything I'd known before. I returned again and again, making acquaintances and eventually friends. My writing life wasn't the same after Word of Mouth.

◆◆◆

Danny Sullivan's New Hampshire restaurant burned down and an arson investigation followed. For a while Danny walked around forlorn and quiet. The cause of the fire deemed inconclusive, Danny received his money and became his old arrogant self again belittling underlings with an air of absolute supremacy. He, Chub, and Gravy got on fabulously. Danny had a nose for cocaine and moved quantity now and again.

Business slowly slipped in the dining room. The food remained good and consistent but people weren't coming. We filled on Friday and Saturday nights but not like the old days. Early in the week the nights could be desolate. The bar was constantly busy. Friday or Sunday, Tuesday or Saturday, they came—the old regulars and the new—friends and acquaintances of Chub and Danny. Gambling was rampant. They made bets with a bookie named Patty, one of the new regulars. They watched every game. Commented loudly to themselves and others. Yelled and banged their hands on the bar if a play didn't go their way. They argued which one of them knew the most about sports.

It drove them crazy that I cared nothing for sports. An important game would be on and behind the bar I paid no attention. They gossiped that I was secretly gay even though I was married. Then they would accuse me of being some kind of snob because I'm a writer. I tried to explain many writers are sports fans.

Name one.

Hemingway.

He don't count he killed himself.

Some sports fan.

The Faggot.

Things went on this way for about a year. Dining room sales continued to slide and I wondered how Chub and Danny were keeping it afloat. Meanwhile they showed no signs of worry and continued partying in the lounge and going to games and eating big meals. I don't know how Chub's wife put up with it, Chub out and about seven days and nights a week. Cash seemed plentiful and Chub spent it. He kept away from any more extramarital activity, but Danny kept two full time girlfriends and neither of them knew about the other.

The first time the police raided The Public Library they found a large sum of unaccounted for cash in the safe. They also found a small amount of pot, Chub's personal stash. They handcuffed Chub in the middle of service and took him through the dining room. Chub taunted the police as they took him, calling them names and warning they'll be sorry. Danny was away at the time and when he returned he was brought in too. Their attorney began working an angle with the warrant and accounting for the money. The pot charge would be minor if they didn't throw it out. Everything went Chub and Danny's way. The case never went to trial. But publicly it sealed the fate of The Public Library. What little business we had left immediately was cut in half.

I didn't know quite what was going on. Chub might act as if he confided in me, but his story shifted with the circumstance so I couldn't believe what he said. It was time for me to get out. I started looking around and calling friends. Then one night about four months after the first raid the police came again. Chub had taken a delivery of pot that afternoon. In his office closet they found twenty-five pounds of weed in vacuum-packed bags. Forty thousand unaccountable dollars were in the safe. Danny had a personal stash of about a half an ounce of cocaine on him, and a pistol for which he had no permit. This finished the restaurant, but Danny held a card. If Danny would fink out a major cocaine dealer and help set him up—Danny and Chub would go free.

♦♦♦

Tulips is a different restaurant since the expansion. Tearing down the wall between the old restaurant and the auto parts store means we have two and a half times the seating capacity. Tabletops that were once bare now feature white tablecloths. Our uniforms go to black and whites from jeans and a casual shirt. The clientele is strictly upscale now and menu prices have increased though the food is good and no one's complaining. People come more than ever.

One significant change is a full liquor license. Originally we served only wine and beer. Expansion brought a custom made cherry wood bar. Now on any given night the bar buzzes with professionals drinking trendy drinks and eating Ed's food. They spend money and generally tip well. Hard liquor's back in a wave of boutique vodkas and new fad drinks.

Tulips' new dining room feels too big for me to work. Or maybe I'm slowing down. The kitchen sits on one side of the place and the bar on the other. The waiter station's located in the back and often I can't see half of my section from the other half or keep track of what's going on. There are more steps to the system and some nights on the floor I do nothing but walk fast in large circles never catching up. In the old place I could see the entire dining room from anywhere in the restaurant. The waiter station was convenient, the kitchen and bar right near each other. Now with more space to cover there must be more servers working. This means less money for everyone to divide in the pool every night. While business has boomed since Tulips expanded, waiter income has dropped.

That's why I prefer the bar where I receive a larger hourly wage and make better tips that I don't have to pool, but it's not easy. The new bar customer is more informed than ever. People want to talk with me about what kind of vodkas we carry and the different flavors. They want to show off their knowledge about wine, ask to look at bottles and seek conversation.

Have you tried this Merlot?

Oh yes, very nice. Customers like it.

The 2001 is delicious, but I haven't tried the 2002s.

Some say it's better.

Hard to beat that concentrated fruit of the 2001s.

Sometimes the differences can be so subtle.

How's that Australian Cabernet?

Big and chewy.

Any suggestions?

The Barolo.

There's no place to go when you are behind the bar. Usually dining room customers don't care to talk much and even if they do you can always avoid the table. Folks who sit at the bar talk. If it isn't about drinks it's about the menu or how long we have been here and how good the food is every time they come. We talk about weather, sports, approaching holidays. As some folks have become regulars over the years, we talk about more personal things like jobs, family and vacations. It's fine when I am in the mood but when not, to face hours on end with people needing to eat and drink, to make conversation and be entertained, it's more than I can take. I count down the time. Two weeks left. Three shifts per week that's six shifts to go.

◆◆◆

I received a phone call from a waiter who previously worked at The Public Library. We'd become friends and went out to a few rock and roll shows together but lost touch as is the case in the business. Chris worked at a hot new place in Copley Square. The last we'd spoken he was making an enormous amount of money. Chris said that the money wasn't quite what it used to be and it was a crazy place to work, but they needed a bartender. It would mean working lunches, which up to then I'd always avoided. But I could squeeze them into doubles and have an extra day per week free for writing. Thus began my short tenure at The Seafood Emporium at Copley Plaza.

Never did I encounter a ship on a sinking course like The Seafood Emporium. The owner was an exceptionally tall Swede named Sven. For nearly a year The Seafood Emporium had been the talk of the local restaurant community. Located in a brand new state of the art mall, situated amongst elite retailers, the upwardly mobile swarmed there to shop and dine. But new malls were opening everywhere and so were restaurants. In a matter of two years The Seafood Emporium became just another place while the mall's clientele changed to tourists and suburban people paying over-priced tags.

Sven drank and drugged hard. Eleven-fifteen in the morning speaking in a deep-throated thick Swedish accent he'd say Joe make me a rum and coke. He liked them strong. The first time I made him a rum and coke he came around the bar and poured it down the sink. Then he refilled the glass with ice, splashed a bit of coke and poured on the rum. This is the way I drink them he said. On a bender he returned after lunch to check if there's any cash in the drawer. If so he cleaned it out. Sven might disappear for several hours, not that he was missed because he didn't do anything but cause problems. He could be out of the building or holed up in his office behind a locked door. Sven might return early evening during dinner hours seating people without a clue of the hostesses seating plan and going in the kitchen to yell at the chef.

Right from the start I hated working lunches. The money was short and during serving hours I had to run double time, a two-hour frenzy. You filled up fast then everyone leaves at once. I had to be at The Emporium at 10:30 in the morning. This meant leaving home around 9:45. After a busy lunch I restocked the bar and had about an hour to myself before I had to get ready for dinner shift. I wandered the mall, window-shopping at endless specialty shops, jewelers, exotic toy stores, expensive men's shoe and clothing retailers and posh women's stores. Air in the mall tasted manufactured and as cold as the surroundings. Time wound slowly as I made my rounds. Often I went back to the The Emporium out of boredom.

The waiters in the dining room were gay and alcoholic. They dragged themselves to work in the morning, turning the coffee machine on as soon as they arrived, eyes bloodshot, disheveled, hands shaking as they poured their first cup. These weren't college-age kids or even thirty-somethings but forty-five year olds with their skin wrinkling and hairlines receding. Some forced a laugh and used humor to feel better. Others were absolute bitches and you avoided them until after the lunch rush. One guy always described his previous night's sexual romp as we set up. During the break between lunch and dinner they went to a local bar and drank spending whatever tips they made from lunch. They'd arrive for dinner shift beaming and when the shift was finished go out to the bars and party.

The idea that I had to be behind a bar from ten-thirty in the morning to eleven at night didn't set right with me. I could have made a good deal of money working a double at The Seafood Emporium, but things had changed and I was barely eking out a night's pay for all my efforts. I knew I wouldn't continue long there but I wanted to take my time finding a better job so I wouldn't put myself in a position like this again. Except for my old acquaintance Chris there weren't even co-workers whom I liked. The waiters were either too hungover or drunk to establish any real contact and the kitchen crew was the most hostile group I've ever encountered. Simply walking through the swinging doors drew hostility from anyone wearing checkered pants, white shirt and a hat.

♦♦♦

Dishwashers are a cult unto themselves. Usually they come and go. The position is a revolving door of faces passing through for a week, two weeks, one night. A dependable dishwasher is as important to any restaurant owner as a good bartender, waiter, or cook—there are more of the later available. Dishwashing isn't complicated but a job of endurance. It's sloppy, wet, and the pay is low for the hours on end rinsing dishes and glasses, placing them into racks, running them through the washer then stacking them on shelves when dry. Kitchen pans must be scrubbed by hand and silverware sorted from bus trays, rinsed and washed. The chef always has some shrimp to clean or potatoes to peel during down time and at the end of the night the dish area must be scrubbed clean and mopped. If someone throws up in the bathroom, the dishwasher cleans it. At the end of the night he is the last to punch out. I say he because in twenty-five years I've only known one female dishwasher. Martha was a young Salvadoran woman who worked at The Central Bistro. She stood five feet tall, was broad, strong and worked as hard as any man.

Sammy is the greatest dishwasher I have known. Working seven years at Tulips he's never missed a shift. As Tulips grows there's been talk of needing a second dishwasher. Sammy tells Ed there's no need. Friday and Saturday nights he does the work of two men, never buckling under pressure and our demands for water glasses, wine glasses, salad plates, cook pans, silverware. Sammy is from El Salvador. I don't know if he is legal. It's hard to tell since so many of the kitchen workers have forged documentation. There is an underground of people who help them do it, for a price. Sammy has certain phrases he is fond of repeating. I walk past him and the man who is usually silent might suddenly blurt out that sometimes life is good sometimes life is bad. On a good night you hear Sammy laughing out loud during a conversation with himself in the kitchen.

Dishwashers have evolved over the years. Always a job open to the most recent immigrants, occasionally high school students, or even a recently released convict on some special program, found their way into the trade. Now dishwashing is below most American high school students. There aren't any more of the programs trying to integrate prisoners back into the workforce. So immigrants, legal and not, make up the hundreds of thousands of dishwashers across the country.

I remember two high school kids at The Public Library who washed dishes for about two months. Gravy named them Cheech and Chong. They smoked copious amounts of weed, brought a big bong to the restaurant and hid it on the back porch where they snuck to fine tune. They were good workers and if one of them didn't show up, the other did. Then one day one of them phoned Gravy and said they quit and sorry they couldn't give notice but they wouldn't be in that night. Gravy, angered, unloaded every one of his great insults. The kid said the bong was still on the porch, could he come in and get it. Gravy told him don't bother, by the time he got there the bong would be in a thousand pieces. The kid never came; Gravy smashed the bong.

At Boylston Bistro the dishwashers were Columbians. They spoke very little English and like Sammy, loved to listen to rock and roll while they worked. Whether or not they were directly involved or just passing it along, word in the Bistro was that they could get the best cocaine around. When I saw waiters and bartenders communicating with them it wasn't difficult to figure out what was going on. One month several hundred dollars were charged to the restaurant phone. The calls were made to Columbia. The dishwashers denied it but they were the only Columbian employees and were let go.

The dishwasher at Tapas, a strapping Argentine, worked as a laborer by day. Gato was always in a good mood and most of the time he worked he whistled. He drank Sangria left in pitchers. Reeling by mid-evening he never missed a beat at that dishwasher. Gato spoke no English and I learned to communicate with him by hand and face signals on matters of silverware, glasses and plates. When Gato finished around one in the morning he bicycled home two cities away. The next morning he rose at six to be to his laborer job at seven.

♦♦♦

The Seafood Emporium split in two with the formal dining

room located inside and the café section in the mall. Shoppers walked by as you served. Food in the café was casual fair the menu priced accordingly. If you looked closely inside the dining room you could see that the once pristine room showed signs of wear. Paint was fading, carpets wearing, an occasional bulb burned out and not replaced. At night this could be disguised with lights low, candle glow on white tablecloths—wine glass glisten. Just under the surface things crumbled.

There were shortages of supplies that made it impossible to set up the dining room completely because the waiters never had enough glassware or silverware. When busy there weren't enough plates to get the food out so busboys ran around clearing plates and running them directly to the dishwasher one at a time. We never had a full bar because there wasn't enough stock. A huge wine and liquor room stood practically empty, as did the kitchen storage area, the freezer and walk-in fridge. Sven didn't pay his bills and when he did he bounced checks. No one in town would give him credit. If liquor, food or supplies arrived nothing came off the truck without a cash payment first.

Mice overran the place. Day or night the little furry things darted from under one table to another. It was something to see the look on diners' faces as they ate overpriced lobster in a restaurant rated highly by *Zagat*, and suddenly realized a mouse ran under their table. If they complained to the hostess or manager, they were told that there was nearby construction and the digging caused the problem. There were people coming in that very night to deal with the situation we were told to say but I never saw exterminators in my tenure at The Emporium.

We went through one manager after another. I worked at The Seafood Emporium for six months and saw four managers pass through. You could see it in their eyes. First an early glow then two weeks later deer in the headlight eyes a few more weeks they're gone. How could one manage Sven's restaurant? There was nothing to manage. The staff's a bunch of drunks and addicts. Several of the waiters were caught doing some kind of credit card scam on the machine. Before he came to The Seafood Emporium the head chef was a pastry chef at a hotel in the Midwest. The clientele was rapidly declining both in numbers and class of people and Sven, a madman, stole every cent of income he could get his hands on. Managers faced three and four crises at once hour after hour.

Sometimes Sven came out of his office and annoyingly made his way around the restaurant ranting about things that made little sense. Correcting me on the proper way to pour a draft beer. Chasing the busboy down to tell him he could get more than that on his tray. Scolding a waiter about the cleanliness of his shirt. He'd take over at the hostess station and seat people without any plan so that one waiter would have five parties and another would have none. If he was too drunk he simply sat down in a chair and passed out, his long legs stretched out in front of him, his tall upper body hunched over, his face barely visible, the deep honks of his snores. Hostesses avoided whatever section Sven went down in and shifted the waiters around accordingly. Sven might wake up at some point during the evening, come to the bar for a glass of ice water and disappear without a word to his office. Other times he remained asleep and we closed up and left him there.

The food at The Seafood Emporium could only be described as fair to bad. Tourists love lobster and we had plenty of it. Broiled, boiled and stuffed along with scallops, shrimp, sole, swordfish, bluefish and a raw bar. Usually we were out of a number of dishes on the menu depending on what Sven was unable to pay for that morning. The kitchen also served the café so the cooks grilled cheeseburgers along side top dollar plates. When busy the cook-line would be a mish-mash of food with café and dining room waiters shuffling around for their items. Chef Nate, or Dessert Chef Nate as he was called, paid little or no attention to seeing the menu into execution. Chef Nate spent hours creating an over-the-top dessert for a special that night. These inventions were often so complex that Chef Nate could only make a dozen or two and the item would sell out by early evening. Then he would float around the dining room and flirt with a hostess and shop in the mall while the cook line slowly ran out of food and sank into the weeds. The cooks yelled and swore at each other; they did the same to the servers.

One morning I arrived to work a double shift. I knew immediately something was abuzz. Sven was under investigation for stealing money from employee payroll deductions earmarked for health insurance. No one was quite certain how he did this. Rumor had it that the restaurant could close or be shut down any day, though the manager assured us it would all work out. On my way in to work that morning I had been thinking of how much I loathed working at The Emporium. I had no friends there. The lack of stock or support made it impossible for anything to go smoothly. I didn't like the clientele and felt demoralized each time I walked through the door. Then it hit me clear as a glass of water. I had nothing to lose. Walk out now.

♦♦♦

Late September air brisk the sun shone down from thick blue sky. People hurried up and down the Boston Public Library stairs as I made my way down Dartmouth Street toward the subway stop. I wondered did I do the right thing walking on the spot? What if I can't find a job? What if The Seafood Emporium won't give me a good reference because I walked? Out the corner of my eye I saw it. I'd noticed the place before but never close enough to read the name. I crossed the street and walked a block down Boylston to the Boylston Bistro.

I walked around to an outside seating area where a waiter stacked dishes on a bus tray. Peak lunch hour wasn't the time to apply for a waiter job so I walked a few doors down for a cup of coffee and a pastry. I drank a second cup to kill more time. Around two I returned to find the same waiter cleaning his near-empty section and asked if they might be hiring. He wasn't sure but kindly brought me inside and found me an application. The manager had left for errands so the waiter took the application and assured me he would pass it along.

Later in the afternoon the manager of Boylston Bistro phoned me. One of the references I put down on my application was Dennis Peters. He was the general manager at The Public Library at one time. We always got along and he liked my work. Unbeknownst to me, Boylston Bistro had recently opened a second, suburban location where Dennis was general manager. Dennis gave me a rave reference. They only had a few shifts available at the present time but he'd be happy to put me on and he was certain things would open up. As always in the restaurant business you can start at a place with one night a week and in no time be working full time—if only picking up shifts other waiters don't want or can't work.

There was one drawback: lunches. The Bistro served

lunch and all waiters were required to work two per week. I chose to do mine in doubles. It made no sense to waste a day going into town, running around madly for several hours, and making thirty dollars. Lunch menus were priced much lower than dinner menus, and lunch diners drank less. The average check was at least half a dinner check and people tended to tip less sober and in daylight. Working lunches was something I had to do—paying dues. Restaurants certainly couldn't profit from it. Many owners opened more as a convenience to customers and to generate more dinner business and what didn't sell as the dinner special one night ended up a lunch special the next day, a good way to get rid of borderline food.

I arrived early my first training morning. The only person around was the bartender setting up. We introduced ourselves. His name was Allen. He said things were a bit casual around the Bistro and I might pour myself a coffee and relax someone would be along soon. Better yet, he asked did I want a glass of champagne. He lifted up a half filled glass and said this new house pour was quite nice, and took a sip. At ten-fifteen I opted for coffee. Around ten-thirty waiters and waitresses began to appear. None of them seemed in any hurry to get to work. They gossiped and drank coffee until eleven then began their various set-ups. I followed a waiter around for two days and after that I was on my own.

Boylston Bistro served French bistro style food: veal, duck, chicken, or seafood selections with the usual array of sauces and reductions. Good food, not great. Serge the chef drank huge icy martinis when the shift wound down. By the time he sat at the bar to finish his paper work he was floating. The general manager also drank. Tim started on Black Russians around nine even though we closed at ten. Tim drove a vintage sports car of some kind and he and Serge shared a house out in the suburbs. They'd stay at the Bistro till one or two in the morning drinking then get into Tim's car and drive home.

Tim always came in the next day wearing a smile. A naturally funny guy, he'd done stand-up comedy and once sang lead in a rock band. Tim arrived, immediately went into a song or a joke. Trailing behind him came Serge, eyes swollen and cigarette dangling from his mouth, no communication he set up his station in pain. The owner didn't seem to notice or care. Hank Dell came in about mid-morning and poked around, never doing much. Near the end of lunch he sat down at the bar and ate. The glass of wine he drank with lunch turned into a brandy and coffee, then a second. He sipped his brandy, smoked cigarettes, and talked with wine salesman making their rounds. Usually he was on his way home by the time we were finished with our first dinner seating.

Small and thin, Hank Dell wore non-descript suits and smoked heavily. He'd been working in the restaurant business since he began as a waiter decades previous. During the 1960s he was a bit of a political radical but was now a conservative businessman. Maybe because he'd worked as a waiter, Hank treated us well and we liked him. He had an unwritten generosity about him. People in the restaurant community felt the same way because Hank did a lot of charity work around town. One time I was smoking a joint on the fire escape overlooking the alley behind the Bistro. The door I'd left ajar slipped shut and I was locked out. I hesitated then knocked on the door. Hank opened it. He said hello and the next day called me aside. I feared I was finished. He twirled his mustache about and asked could I get him some grass.

♦♦♦

Eventually the Word of Mouth Reading Series offered me a feature reading. My poetry had evolved, new friends and acquaintances I made at Word of Mouth were supportive, and I realized that I was beginning to write poems of my own.

I finished my first novel and called it *Tending*. Soon I began to contact agents and publishers, with no success. As time passed I got discouraged. As my ideas of what a poem could be expanded I now saw my novel as conventional with nothing original or remarkable about it. I wrote the novel the way I had learned a novel should be written. My dialogue bore nothing special—neither did the narrative technique. I decided to shelve the manuscript. Perhaps I wasn't a novelist after all. My poetry was bringing a modicum of success and that is where I would put my energy. Poems were being accepted by various little magazines. After my reading at Word of Mouth I gave readings at other venues around the city. Friendships developed with writers I came in contact with. If it took working shifts in a restaurant at night to support this new life, so be it. While I was fortunate enough to befriend some older and established writers, the majority of us were newcomers trying to find our way. We met for drinks or coffee, talking poetry, art, music and politics. Soon a group of us began meeting on Monday nights at our Somerville apartment. Calling ourselves the Dante Group, we read Dante's *Divine Comedy* in its original Italian, drinking wine and eating snacks until late hours.

All of us were achieving some success with poems published now and again, but we felt that we needed more. I decided to take a cue from what my new friend Michael Franco, who also made his living as a waiter, had done with his Word of Mouth Series. The idea of starting a little magazine of my own had been in the back of my mind and it was time to put it out front. With Molly's help I soon began to publish *lift*, a magazine of poetry, prose and art. I collected work from many writers and artists with whom I had become friends. Soon we were bringing out four issues per year from our apartment. I did the editing, Molly helped out with the design and production in addition to contributing artwork. No sooner did we get one issue out, I began collecting work for another. I arrived home at night from a shift, opened a beer and sat down with whatever manuscripts might have come in the mail, enjoying a kind of satisfaction I had never known.

♦♦♦

Betty Ann worked seven days a week when Tulips first opened. She did the books and worked the door seating people at night but since the expansion she has taken much less of a role in the front of the house. She and Ed hired a general manager, more hostesses and a part-time accountant who Betty Ann supervised.

I don't see her for several days suddenly she appears inspects the waiter stations and bar area. Occasionally she visits during dinner hours. Then she walks around straightening piles of menus, re-arranging bar napkins, rotating the bar fruit from cherries, olives, oranges, limes and lemons to lemons, limes, oranges, cherries and olives. In the waiter station she re-stacks coffee mugs and checks to see there is enough tea stocked or picks up the drip pan on the espresso machine to look underneath and see that it is clean. It's her restaurant.

Betty Ann was originally a kindergarten teacher but with budget cuts came fewer jobs and she eventually went back to working as a waitress like she had in college. Eventually she met Ed, a rock and roll guitarist who left college for cooking school. They took a lot on with the expansion. Rumor has it they have their house on the line. It cost more to do the new construction than it did to open the restaurant. But business has been good and the extra space allows for a private dining room and functions are on the increase.

The full bar license has brought the new martini crowd in droves. But as Ed points out, doubling the size means double the heating, air-conditioning and water bills and increased payroll. Tulips is a success story. We get good reviews, word of mouth is a constant, and all along Mass. Ave. new places are opening in Arlington as a result of Tulips doing well. No matter the competition, our clientele returns and new faces appear all the time.

♦♦♦

As the wine industry has grown, so has the number of wine salesmen. They always have the latest wine given a 95 in *The Wine Spectator,* or a fabulous first time blend or recent release. During the afternoon they line up saying hello as they pass each other, Lou the bar manager sampling one person's wares while another salesman eavesdrops. Lou buys from a handful of people and warns solicitors that his list is fine right now. If he has time and a salesperson persists Lou gives them a few minutes. On Wednesday afternoons Lou does most of his tasting. He sits at the bar with dozens of glasses and a pitcher of water and a champagne bucket to spit in.

There are so many varieties and blends of wine it is

impossible to keep up. Soon as I learn of one new estate or wine there are three others. All of the world vineyards are producing wine from traditional cabernet sauvignons and chardonnays to some of the most esoteric fusions. Vines in Italy are being transported and grown in California. There's a wine estate in Rhode Island. Every local liquor store has wine tastings. Like any product be it cars or stereos, the key is to keep it new. People no longer want good Chianti, instead they want a "Super Tuscan." I call them Stupid Tuscans. Or maybe they aren't so stupid, considering the prices they demand for their new designer Italian wines.

Occasionally if a wine company is doing a promotion the salesperson will bring their manager along. In some instances they will appear with the owner of an estate who is touring to promote his wine: well-dressed mild-mannered northern Italians, wealthy yuppies from California, a big, strapping New Zealander who nearly broke my hand when he shook it. Each of them has a story. It is the story of their wine and what makes it so special. Lou handles them well and does most of his business with people he likes. Everybody's got some kind of deal it's a matter of who you choose to support.

♦♦♦

More artists were employed at Boylston Bistro than any place I ever worked. There were musicians, actors, writers, female impersonators, photographers, dancers and painters. A mix of gay and straight folks and everyone got along fine. We made good money at night. Dinners went smoothly if we were busy the staff was experienced enough to handle things. But having to be at the mercy of a job from ten-thirty in the morning to eleven-thirty at night wasn't worth the excellent cash that I was making. Working those long days meant needing more down time to rest on days off. Dragging myself to work early, I felt suffocated.

One day Hank pulled me aside to say one of the floor managers had given notice and he wanted to offer me the position. It wasn't as serious as it sounded. Floor manager meant being manager on duty, two lunch shifts and one evening shift per week. Best part was I wouldn't have to serve food any more lunch shifts. The job consisted of setting up the bank, writing and printing the daily menu, seating people as host, dealing with any problems that arose and overseeing the staff. Until that time I never had any desire to work as a manager. Managers often earned less than servers and worked longer hours. But Hank offered me decent money for each manager shift. Moreover I could sit down and dine after the shift and come in for dinner once a month on the house. The shift pay was far more than I could make working a lunch shift and gave me an immediate raise for less time worked all around.

It wasn't difficult being floor manager. Occasionally the kitchen might be late giving me the menu and I had to rush writing it with my bad penmanship. Occasionally a diner sent their dinner or appetizer back or had some other kind of problem and I would go to the table, apologize and find out how we could make it right. The clientele was a mix of tourists and denizens of Boston's Back Bay. Tourists stuck out in their vacation clothes. Local folks dined in expensive but understated dress or casual wear, occupied with their own conversations they desired no interaction with me outside my duties. Tourists wanted to know about me. They wanted to tell me things about themselves. They asked my name and told me theirs. They wanted to talk about the Red Sox and shook my hand on the way out.

I became friendly with the bartender Allen. We shared similar interests in music, politics and books. We talked and disagreed much but it was all good-natured. Allen was a talker. In my years I've never known anyone who could outtalk him. His stories could go ten and fifteen minutes and I might forget what he's talking about in the first place. Allen grew up working in his family's used bookstore and was a passionate reader. At the time Allen applied to law schools for several years in a row but couldn't get admitted. It wasn't that Allen wanted a big law career—hardly—he was a socialist of sorts, interested in law as a way of helping people. Allen had graduated college with so-so grades ten years previous. He wasn't a high profile candidate. Nonetheless the year after I left the Bistro Allen got accepted and went to law school.

It's a transient business. Waiters and bartenders come and go. It's easy to befriend certain folks when working together but it is rare to make long-term friends. However, Allen and I not only became friends but we stayed in contact as he made his way through law school and we remain friends today. He set up practice in Somerville and recently purchased a house three streets away from me.

The Bistro dining room was long and narrow with an outside patio located on the sidewalk. Tourists loved to sit there as busses, trucks and cars chugged along Boylston Street blowing exhaust a few feet away. The tables and chairs were made of plastic and on windy days they blew over and rolled down Boylston. Working the patio was like a sentence. Everything was located in the back of the restaurant. A patio shift meant running back and forth, trip after trip, bringing out food and supplies—returning with dirty dishes and empty pitchers. Pigeons congregated on the ledge directly above and frequently shat on tables, people and food. Once as I took an order a glob of squishy green stuff fell on my head but I continued to take the order as if nothing happened, the two people at the table seemed fine with it.

William had worked at Boylston Bistro since it opened and had more experience as a waiter than any of us. We considered him the uncrowned manager. He kept an eye on the goings-on in the front of the house and kitchen. Hank confided in him and it wasn't uncommon to see them in conference over restaurant details. William expected a certain level of professionalism, and that was fine with me. He was about fifty and had been living with his partner for many years. He had a way of sashaying around that seemed years in the making. A raging queen at twenty he had refined the art to a stately air. He was helpful and capable of sensitive conversation, and fond of telling us about Father Bob, the priest who brought him out. William said that it wasn't abuse—he knew what he was doing—and Father Bob was there to guide him along the way. A shine came over William's eyes when he spoke of Father Bob.

Six months passed and the combination of working a few night shifts as a waiter and three shifts as floor manager worked well for me. The part of managing I liked least was overseeing my coworkers. A few took advantage and slacked off now and again. Having to tell a server lingering in the waiter station that tables needed tending, or scold them for coming in late fueled some ill feelings against me. Nonetheless it was my job. Except for the most obnoxious, tending to diners' problems was painless. I apologized when there was a problem, offered dessert on the house, or took an item off a check. The toughest ones received a gift certificate for dinner on the house. I wore a jacket and tie, seated people, helped the servers if they were in a jam, and at the end of the shift ate dinner and drank a glass of wine.

In time, Tim and Serge's drinking caught up with them. Hank had them both on the carpet over their excesses and for a few weeks everything seemed better. But soon the two were back to their old ways and by the middle of any given evening they were both drunk. Serge's food was okay when under the influence but his plates were sloppy. Tim became a complete lush and stumbled around. Often other servers and I would do our best to keep him out of the dining room so he didn't embarrass himself. One night Hank came in unexpected. He fired them both. Mitchell, Serge's assistant, was given the chef position. A young guy who played in a band, Mitchell had limited experience in kitchens. Hank also hired a new manager. Dale had worked for restaurant chains with no experience in fine dining. Word was out that Hank brought him in to tighten up what he saw as a loose ship.

Mitchell's cooking could be adequate when he stuck to Serge's basic recipes. But he had no sense of balance with his own creations. He over-seasoned, poured too heavy with cream, mixed flavors and textures poorly so there was no place for the palette to settle. His pasta dishes were particularly appalling—one of his favorites was cheese ravioli with calamari in a balsamic vinegar sauce to which he added a touch of cream. Most of the tourists didn't seem to notice and raved about the food. Regulars were soon asking was there a new chef? Hank confided to me because I was a floor manager that he planned on replacing Mitchell as soon as he found an appropriate person. A few weeks later I arrived one morning and Hank introduced me to the new chef. Hank said it was time to change the direction of our cuisine. The new chef focused on the "New American Cuisine" that was becoming the rage. No longer intimidated by the classic cuisine of Europe, the new breed of chef's looked homeward to the produce, and various American traditions.

Dale was a mean-spirited manager. In no time it became clear that Hank brought him in to do his dirty work. Hank looked the other way. Dale pulled servers aside and threatened them with their employment if they didn't straighten out. He was particularly hard on women, especially the younger ones and on several occasions made them cry. During his first month managing he fired three servers. All of them were women performing their jobs fine. Because I was a floor manager Dale treated me well and respected my years of experience. At the same time he expected me to toughen my stance and become more critical of the staff. One day Allen witnessed an incident between Dale and another female server. He called Dale on it in front of the staff. They argued and Dale fired him. Three days later I gave two week's notice.

♦♦♦

Molly, a registered nurse, worked mostly evenings. When possible we worked the same evenings each week. This allowed us time for our art and plenty of time for ourselves. We liked visiting New York City and often spent days tooling around Boston and Cambridge, visiting museums and galleries, seeing movies and going out to clubs to hear music. We enjoyed dining out and took long lunches that melted into afternoon drinks, or hopped around to various good restaurants for dinner.

I continued putting out *lift* and began organizing my first full-length book of poems. Around this time I published my first chapbooks of poetry. They were done in limited edition and read by friends. But it gave me an emotional boost and helped me become more confident as a writer. During this time I had no bad attitude about restaurant work like many of the people I came in contact with—those artists and students who felt it was beneath them, that they deserved better. Any day that I did some writing, editing, lunched with a friend, made it easier to don the apron that night. What else could I be doing that could afford me the luxury of such a life?

My father died around this time. Since our relationship had been strained my feelings were complicated. It wasn't that I mourned his loss—I couldn't lose what I never had. I knew no father and son bond because he was a man unable to connect with the people closest to him. I couldn't forgive him for it. A tortured human being and a victim of his demons, he took it out on his family, especially me. As I grew older and became a writer I might as well have joined the Foreign Legion. As a boy I worked in the gas station he ran in our hometown of Medford. Not long after he died I began dreaming regularly of the gas station. Night after night the people, events, sights and sounds returned to me. My father was at the center of these dreams, often taunting me, and I taunted back, telling him to get out of my life, that he was dead and no longer had any power over me.

Several years later I left Tulips when my first novel *Gas Station* had received considerable critical attention, generating interest in my other finished books. There was a new book deal, a small amount of money, and for the first time I secured a literary agent who promised that she would get me out of waiting tables and I believed her. So with the money dribbling in I figured I could survive until better fortune came my way. Six months later I was broke. The agent had done nothing with my manuscripts. In fact it was clear that she really didn't understand my books. I dropped her and soon found myself back at Tulips looking to be put back on the schedule. Ed and Betty Ann welcomed me back and in no time I was working the floor and the bar as if I'd never left.

This time I don't have the promise of a way out. There isn't an agent or publisher for a writer with books published and no sales. But there is no way I can remain here although Tulips isn't the problem. I don't know of a better restaurant to work. I'm burned out. Exhausted. Can't concentrate. My patience with customers is practically non-existent. I wander around the dining room daydreaming, wondering what will become of me. At fifty years old I have no money saved, no job training nor skills at anything except serving people. I continue to second-guess myself. With nothing on the horizon I'm doomed to return to the business—if not to Tulips than another place. The idea of beginning a new job, being trained by some kid with his nose pierced, getting used to new management and restaurant procedures leaves me ill.

But just coming to work and having to do side-work is enough to reinforce my decision to leave. It's not the stocking glasses, silverware and plates that annoys me. Nor setting up the waiter station, or dining room and having the manager come by and say that one of my tables looks sloppy. The most demoralizing duty is cleaning bathrooms. In all my years I have never worked at a place where waiters didn't have to clean bathrooms. There's toilet paper to stock, mirrors to polish, sinks to clean. Little trashcans that hold women's used sanitary napkins must be emptied. Worst is cleaning the toilets. To get down and scrub out a toilet seems like the biggest irony of all. We serve them the food then clean the toilets where they shit it out. For some reason women are the biggest offenders, leaving their marks stuck on the inside of the bowl. I'm not sure why. Having to scrub those hard-to-remove stains is enough to spoil my staff dinner. Even worse are Sunday night shifts—after a brunch with all the hungover brunch folks swigging Bloody Marys and hot coffee before making their deposits.

The side-work at the end of the shift's a matter of wiping down the waiter station, taking out the trash, and vacuuming the carpet. I do it automatically, tired from the shift but mustering enough energy to get the trash barrel up and toss its contents into the dumpster, or fumbling around the tables to get the main crumbs up from the floor with the vacuum cleaner. Each restaurant I've worked has a different amount of side-work. There are places where servers can remain long after their last diner leaves doing special side-work like polishing brass, washing chairs, wiping down woodwork with oils. Some places have reputations as side-work heavy employers. Unless the money is exceptional, these are places to be ignored. Amongst experienced waiters, word gets around fast in terms of which are the best places to work. Money alone is never the deciding factor. Working conditions and employer temperaments are equally important.

♦♦♦

Tired from going back and forth to Boston and having to work lunches I decided to look closer to home for employment. The face of Somerville changing, new restaurants were opening around town. In nearby Davis Square a Spanish restaurant Tapas had recently opened. One afternoon I took a walk and banged the knocker on the rustic wooden front doors. A woman in her mid-fifties, a bad blonde dye job and hunched over shoulders opened the door. She wore a blue floor length dress that looked out of place and time, like Morocco meets the 1940s. Skin pale and wrinkled she looked in need of sleep. I told her I was looking for work, and she asked how much experience. I told her and she opened the door wider, said come in. I'd heard about Tapas but was not ready for what I found inside.

The place looked like a set from a Fellini movie, exotic lights strung about, dozens of masks and prints of surreal paintings hanging on the hideously painted orange-pink walls. A long clothesline extended the length of the dining room from which multiple articles of women's underwear hung from clothespins. A gold-plated statue of Venus sat on a stand in one corner with red pasties on her nipples. Over the bar the stuffed head of a wild boar with its tusks exposed looked down over the spectacle. There was no place the eye could rest.

Viviana and her husband owned Tapas. She said it's a very special place and they were looking for employees who not only had experience but some kind of charisma too. She told me she liked my ponytail. I took it as a good sign. Viviana asked what else do I do. I told her I was a writer she asked what do I write. Fiction and poetry I said. She made her way behind the bar and told me she loved e.e. cummings and asked did I? To which I responded of course he's one of my favorites. I lied to her. Viviana reached into the wine rack and pulled out a bottle of red. She placed it on the bar with an empty wine glass, handed me a corkscrew and asked me to open the bottle of wine. I picked up the bottle and presented it to her then cut off the foil top, pulled the cork and with the label facing her poured a taste into the goblet. She picked up the glass, nosed the rim and drank it down.

A short stout man with tiny eyes, thin mustache and

shaved head appeared. He wore a brightly flowered shirt with white pants and asked Viviana what was going on. In a forceful voice he spoke English with a Spanish accent. It was Viviana's husband Patricio. She informed him of my inquiry and how I'd just opened a bottle of wine perfectly. He said good someone who knows how to do things right then shook my hand so hard I thought he'd break my pinky. Patricio poured himself a glass of the red, refilled Viviana's glass and asked would I like some. I didn't know how to answer. I'd never been offered a drink on a job interview but one look at the place, Patricio and Viviana I thought best to accept. I told Patricio just a little and he filled my glass.

Patricio drank his wine down as if it were a glass of water and excused himself. Viviana informed me that she liked me but was unable to offer much in terms of work at the time. I could work one night on the bar and one night on the floor to start. Several people she'd hired were not working out and it wouldn't be long until there would be more shifts available. Uncomfortable coming in to a place where I'd be waiting for someone to be fired before I had a schedule, I figured they'd be fired nonetheless and it would only mean someone else would have the job. I asked Viviana if they opened for lunch or did they have any plans for opening lunches. She winced and replied that she and Patricio were night people and the last thing they wanted to do was have the restaurant serve lunch. That cinched it for me and I accepted.

♦♦♦

There's something about getting out of work after midnight, a sense of freedom and alienation. Houses are quiet and dark, flickers of television light behind windows. At the end of a restaurant shift there are two ways to go: home, or out. But it only takes one or two drinks for the adrenaline to kick in.

It doesn't take much for the young folks. Everyone knows the latest last calls and when those establishments close there's always an apartment with beer, wine or pot. Three or four in the morning becomes a regular bedtime. Eleven in the morning or noon is breakfast. These days I have a ginger ale and hop on my bicycle for the slow pedal back to Somerville.

I try to ride my bicycle in throughout the year. Once the snow comes it makes it difficult because of the ice and slush. Frigid temperatures don't stop me, I wear layers of clothing and during hot summer months I slip out of my dress shirt into a t-shirt before I depart. On clear nights I measure phases of the moon and fix my eyes on stars. If it's raining I endure it and pull off my wet clothes when I get home. Along Mass. Avenue there's traffic at any hour but once I cut off to the side streets everything goes silent. Tired when I begin my ride by the time I arrive home my body is exhilarated. My wife and children are sound asleep upstairs. I try to unwind with reading or television.

If the night's been difficult I turn over the various skirmishes in my head. Ed got mad at me for screwing up an order. I had a run-in with a nasty customer and I relive the event over and over in my head. Maybe I am frustrated over another co-worker whose side-work I had to do. These matters are insignificant in the big scheme but in the early morning hours my mind will not let them go. They swirl around my consciousness gnawing at my stomach, preventing me from concentrating on my reading or a particular television program. Eventually I begin to tire, climb the stairs and slide into bed falling to sleep at two or three in the morning.

♦♦♦

Over the years whenever I've found a restaurant that is a good place to work I remained there for a considerable time. Some servers follow the trends and hop from one new hot place to another, making the big cash that flows in when a recently opened eatery catches on. In time business levels off and these people move on to the next new thing. The extra money, the difficulty of changing jobs every six months or year and the uncertainty of new owners, systems and co-workers, never appealed to me. I'd rather make consistent money in an eatery where I feel comfortable. During my twenty-five years I've worked a handful of places that didn't work out from the very beginning and I've left after a very short time. A number of them I don't even remember; others I remember too well.

Uva had recently opened in Boston when I found myself there working my first training shift. I was attracted to the place because it billed itself as an Italian restaurant with an emphasis on fine Italian wines. Over the years I'd developed a passion for Italian red wines such as Barolos, Barbarescos, Brunellos and Amarones. The owners of Uva were a husband and wife team. The two young yuppies had taken several extended vacations in Tuscany. There they reached some kind of epiphany and decided it was their calling to share their love of northern Italy's food and wine with American diners. The wife interviewed me and impressed by my Italian wine and food knowledge hired me.

My first night an eighteen-year-old girl trained me and Uva was her first restaurant job. I asked various questions about procedures she seemed unable to answer. I attempted to talk about wines or food and she knew even less. I didn't know until that first night that the place served pizza. Further, the pasta dishes were ordered by number since the customer decided what kind of sauce or meat they wanted with their linguine or ziti which meant some folks might order Fettucine Alfredo with meatballs and sausage: number fifteen with three, seven, and eight. An hour into the evening the trainer waitress sold a bottle of wine and I offered to open it for her. She informed me that the owner opened all the wine because most of the servers didn't know how. I reminded myself that I would be pooling tips with these children. I walked over to the owner, told him that this was not going to work for me and took the subway home.

The only formal restaurant I ever worked at was The Harvard Room in Harvard Square. We wore black and whites with tuxedo jackets. Before I could work my way onto the dining room floor I was required to do banquet service. This was during peak graduation season. Situated on three floors with the main dining room on the top floor, The Harvard Room had an overflow-dining/banquet room on the second floor and another banquet room on the first floor. The owners were men who seemed frazzled at all times. One of them was such an alcoholic that he openly drank gin and tonics all day long and went around telling us how lucky we were to be getting thirteen dollars an hour while most banquet waiters made twelve.

Setting up a banquet room meant carrying tables and chairs up and down stairs, silverware, plates, glasses, linens and the bar service. One too many times after a two-hour set-up one or both of the owners arrived on the scene and decided that the banquet would be better served on the upper or lower level and we had to completely break down the room and reset everything on another floor with a very short time before the party's arrival. By then the owners were on our backs to hurry or we wouldn't be ready on time. When one of the owners approached me about a position in the regular dining room I declined and left shortly thereafter.

Giordanos was a huge restaurant on Mass. Avenue in Cambridge. Desperate for work I took the position despite the fact that they opened for lunch. As usual I opted to work doubles on lunch shift days to get them out of the way without wasting a day off having to set-up, serve for two hours, then break down for a nominal amount of tips. It took me no time to see Giordanos as the most poorly managed, disorganized, chaotic eatery I ever encountered next to The Seafood Emporium. Up to that time I'd never seen such dishonesty and customer deception. Giordanos's main claim was that most of their produce and meat came from the big farm the company owned about thirty miles west of the city. It took me a few days seeing produce and meat delivered from purveyors to realize that this was a farce. Somehow no one seemed to question this even though on the top of the menu Giordanos's guarantee of freshness from their own farm was the first thing a diner read.

The man who owned Giordanos, Vincent Giordano boasted that he came to this country as a boy with the shirt on his back and a shovel then built a small empire. Indeed besides the restaurant and farm he owned a number of office buildings and a commercial plumbing and heating business worth millions. It was said no matter how low a competitor might bid for a job, Vincent Giordano never missed out on a state contract. I disliked him from the first time I set eyes on him. He looked right through me when the manager introduced us. During dinner hours he would arrive with a woman at least half his age, sit at the bar to eat and drink while he mugged at his young doll. I imagined at home his older Italian wife dutifully waited for him. To prove his power it was not uncommon for him to fire a server or cook on the spot for a minute mistake, often during the middle of a shift.

As for working as a waiter I was on my own. Sections were too large and unmanageable when it got busy. Items on the menu were commonly not available. Wines on the list weren't consistent with the years and labels stated. Other servers paid little attention to side-work so glasses, silver and other supplies were not stocked and I frequently found myself chasing around for a fork, wine glass or water pitcher. Busboys spoke no English. Ask one for something and he'd disappear return ten minutes later hands empty. The coffee station was never set-up and stocked properly and the espresso machine so broken down the cappuccino and espresso were barely drinkable.

The kitchen staff was psycho with cooks fighting amongst themselves and with the waiters. One lunch shift I went to pick up food later than the chef thought I should have. He screamed at me to pick up the fucking food and called me a moron. I warned him not to speak to me that way and he threw both dishes in question to the kitchen floor, globs of sauce and pasta landed on my shoes and the bottom of my pants. I left the kitchen walked down to the manager's office where I tossed my checks, the money I'd collected and my apron on his desk. I told him I was leaving and wouldn't be back.

You can't just leave in the middle of shift.

Just watch me.

You're on the schedule tonight.

That's your problem.

I won't give you a reference.

I wouldn't tell my dog I worked in this shit hole.

◆◆◆

I met Lou at Tapas, and we've been working together at various establishments ever since. He trained me on the floor because he was the only one who spoke English. We hit it off immediately. Lou was a playwright at the time starting up a theater company that would produce plays from Boston-area writers. Lou was gay but one of those hard to tell guys. He disliked queens saying if he wanted a woman he would be straight.

In addition to my training and orientation Lou gave me the ins and outs of working at Tapas. He warned that Patricio could be a bully towards employees and capable of temper tantrums. Viviana was worse. Patricio had been in the restaurant business for years and carried that experience with him. Viviana was a barfly at the restaurant Patricio once managed. The two became friendly and eventually Patricio left his wife of thirty years for her. Shortly thereafter the two opened Tapas with Patricio's money. Viviana loved her role as an owner. Lou told me I was better off having Patricio yell at me over something he deemed wrong than have Viviana chase me over things she new nothing about. Why I didn't read the handwriting then and find another job I'll never know.

A short, sweet Columbian man named Jorge trained me on the bar. Tapas was his first restaurant job and while he knew the bar system, his inexperience showed when it was busy as he lagged behind. Jorge was friendly, unlike the waiters and waitresses who gave me a cold shoulder from the beginning and considered me a Gringo. Lou spoke a little Spanish while I knew not a word. No one in the kitchen spoke English and several of the cooks were illiterate. You had to order verbally like "Pulpo," or "Queso Asado," or "Gambas."

Nights I worked the bar Patricio and Viviana were pleased with my performance. As a server I was plagued with the worst sections, low-balling diners, and Patricio and Viviana nagging me throughout the shift. There were times when I didn't get seated until the Hispanic servers had nearly full sections, so I was always at least one turn behind and made considerably less at the end of the night. Further, Hispanic servers got the regulars and customers who were known for spending big money. Once the place was filled Patricio ran around the dining room pushing us to turn over tables, yelling for us to give him tables he needed tables as the people waiting to get seated lined out the door. It was utter chaos with Patricio's shouting, Viviana's badgering, the fast pace, loud Hispanic music blaring through the stereo and customers wild from the atmosphere and too much Sangria.

Diners raved enthusiastically all the way out the door about Tapas's second-rate food. This was due mostly to Tapas's festive décor and the potent Sangria turning the squarest of the squares into hipper than hips. A long list of tapas, or small appetizer-portions made up the greater part of the menu and became Tapas's signature. These so-called delicacies were overpriced and the portions were minuscule. They were prepped en masse during the day. The sheer volume that the kitchen produced on a given night limited any cooking-to-order. Microwave ovens lined the kitchen walls and many an item found its way into them.

People praised the goat cheese tapas—a slab of goat cheese on top of a bland tomato sauce. The tuna stuffed squid with black ink sauce contained squid stuffed with canned tuna with a dollop of black ink sauce cooked in the microwave. Garlicky chicken featured tiny pre-cooked chicken overloaded with garlic, also warmed in the microwave. Garlicky shrimp were tiny flavorless shrimp doused with too much olive oil and too much garlic. Grilled chorizo was only a few slices of the dried, tough sausage placed in the little bowl. What seemed at first like a reasonably priced meal quickly added up once diners ordered a second or third round of tapas.

Entrées were overpriced and none bore any culinary merit to speak of. Chicken, beef, lamb or rabbit, sauces were too rich and over-flavored. It was impossible to taste any meat underneath such over-the-top preparations of sherry, wines, ports, cream and too many herbs and spices. Paella had a faint metallic taste from the pans in which it was prepared. Patricio insisted that these were the traditional pans for preparing Paella and simply dismissed an occasional complaint as coming from an American who didn't know any better. The entrée that topped all others in popularity was the salt cooked fish. A whole fish was packed in salt and cooked in the oven, placed in a wooden box that we carried to the table. At the table we set the box on a stand, broke the salt off the fish and cut off the filets to the oohs and ahhs of the diners. The fish should have been moist and flavorful, instead it was dry and flavorless. An uninspired coriander sauce came on the side.

♦♦♦

After my father died my mother sold her house and she gave us the down payment for our own home. Molly and I found a small single family around the corner from the apartment we'd occupied for ten years—but not without some problems securing a mortgage. I made plenty of money in the business, but only a fraction of it legal and on paper. My tax records showed that I made about a hundred and fifty dollars per week. In actuality I made at least triple that amount since Tapas only accepted cash and I could bury much of my income. The bank kept us hanging an excessive amount of time claiming the amount we asked for wasn't up to our income. They knew that I made more than it appeared but it didn't matter. In all my years serving, every penny I could gyp the government out of I considered well earned. For the first time the effects of this kind of money making had a double-edge. Eventually the bank gave in. We secured a mortgage and moved in to our first home.

Ultimately the publication of *lift* began to wind down. It seemed that I had taken the production as far as it needed to go. I decided that we would do a series of little books by poets who were frequent contributors to the magazine, four in all. Then I put the *lift* project to rest after sixteen issues and four books. I thought it time for me to move on. My first manuscript of poetry completed I began to look for a publisher.

It was about that time I had a vision of *Gas Station*. One pleasant Sunday afternoon I walked down Somerville Avenue on my way to a reading at Word of Mouth. I passed a gas station and the smell of gas wafting about struck me in a profound way. Suddenly memories of my own days at my father's station began to swirl around my head, in no linear manner but fleeting glimpses stirring me emotionally, the way an unexpected scent, or song on the radio can ignite. Imagine that I thought to myself, to catch those unexpected twirling recollections down on paper.

♦♦♦

Years ago restaurants featured predictable menus. You found steaks, chops, prime rib. Baked stuffed shrimp, baked haddock or scallops with butter, wine and breadcrumbs. Who can forget surf and turf? Wine selections were slim: French and a few Italian reds. Cocktails consisted of martinis, manhattans, whiskey sours and old fashioneds. It seems like long ago and it is.

Now the upscale eateries are omnipresent, downtown Boston to the far reaches of the suburbs, slick dining rooms and wine bars rule. Cooking schools turn out graduates like sausages from a machine, all of them holding to the dream of owning their own bistro, getting reviewed, having photos of themselves appear with their recipes in the dining sections of the newspapers. Chefs have become celebrities. The better-known one becomes, the higher his or her rating. Many chefs hire public relations people in order to maintain their public persona. It's as if food has become second behind reputation. Diners flock to the restaurants where the stars practice their art, many simply to be seen and perhaps have a word with the chef.

No matter how talented a cook there is only so much one can do with food. The mass of new eateries rotates variations on the same themes. You still find steaks and chops, but now it's a flank steak with gorgonzola butter, crispy onion rings, garlicky mashed potatoes and some kind of exotic greens. Pork chops are cured, served with a maple glaze, mashed sweet potatoes and collard greens. Lamb is braised with chile peppers, beer, and southwestern spices and tossed with pasta. There's always salmon, maybe with baby new potatoes over a bed of fancy greens dressed with raspberry vinaigrette. Scallops are no longer broiled or baked but pan seared and topped with an Asian-flavored drizzle. As the old North Atlantic white fish have disappeared fish like skate have appeared, a ray fish whose wings are removed and floured, sautéed and served with a tomato butter sauce over a risotto. There's mahi mahi, John Dory, sturgeon. On any given menu various manifestations of these items can be found. Like spaghetti and meatballs, lasagne or veal parmesan in some red sauce Italian joint.

Ed came up the hard way and has carefully avoided the star chef status coveted by so many of his contemporaries. His ingredients are fresh, yet steers away from the trendier elements of this new cuisine. When he can he buys produce and meat from area farmers rotates his menu every six weeks. Wines from around the world comprise the wine list and every season a new cocktail becomes the rage and we must carry the alcohol necessary for the ingredients. At the bottom of these new concoctions is the liquor industry, ever-seeking to increase their take on the market.

I'm sick of it. If I shake one more trendy drink, look at one more piece of grilled salmon, one dish of pumpkin ravioli with a sage cream sauce, it will be too soon. I'm counting down the days.

♦♦♦

Greed kept me at Tapas. Six months into my employment I was moved permanently to the bar. This worked fine for me the money would be better. The doors opened at six and by six-thirty on any night the bar was full and we worked flat out until midnight. No sooner did one party leave after tapas, Sangria and sherry another group took its place. A bell hung over the sherry and port bottles we rang when someone left a big tip. Jorge and I made a good match. He usually served the Spanish speakers who made up a fair amount of the clientele, while I waited on the yuppies, tourists, and academics from nearby Harvard who often expressed disappointment that I wasn't Spanish.

Funny, you look Spanish.

No, Italian.

Well, close enough.

I made as much money working the bar as I've ever made but it was physically and mentally draining. Set-up began at 3:30. There was lots of daily cleaning. Patricio and Viviana demanded everything be cleaned and polished, from the bar and stools to all the bottles and glasses. We had to empty out the beer coolers and wipe out the insides. We made Sangria in five-gallon drums: red wine, brandy, sugar and fruit that we mixed with a big wooden paddle. The Sangria containers were stored in the basement cooler. To do this we went into the kitchen, dodging busy waiters and cooks, climbing down a set of narrow wooden stairs, then back up. By the end of the night, my back ached from the endless cases of beer, drums of Sangria, and cases of wine. Full on the way up, empty on the way down.

Viviana and Patricio rode us the entire evening. Patricio used us as his punching bag for things going wrong. He might appear yelling there's a case of empty beer left at the bottom of the stairs or we weren't rotating the Sangria. Usually it wasn't true but there was never a thing we could say or do. Patricio had a sign on his office desk that read No Excuses. And he accepted none, no matter the situation. Viviana drove us endlessly mad with little things that had nothing to do with overall bar operations. Jorge and I were completely competent and no two people could do more under the circumstances. No matter how petty, her myriad demands had to be met. Viviana kept a public note board in the kitchen. On any given day she posted notes for all to see—who's shirt needed washing, another could use some mouthwash, and who must speed up his service or get smaller sections.

Viviana would tell us to do something this way, and Patricio told us the opposite. Place five stacks of bar napkins every two stools. Place four stacks of bar napkins every two and a half stools. Fill a glass of wine two-thirds of the way. Fill a glass of wine slightly more than one-half of the way. Slice two pieces of bread per person. Slice three pieces of bread per person. Have the wait staff cash out before they do end-of-the-night side-work. Have them cash out after side-work is finished. Begin stocking the bar when it slows down late. Wait until after last call to restock the bar. Fill the Sangria pitchers all the way to the top with ice. Fill the pitchers three-quarters of the way with ice. It went on and on like this. Viviana asked why we weren't doing something the way she told us. Patricio yelled at us that he'd already said how he wanted it done. There was nothing I could say. Neither would listen.

The two of them were serious drinkers. They went out for lunch and soused themselves with wine and cocktails. After lunch Viviana went home and didn't return until half an hour before we opened. Usually she'd just woken from a nap and in a foul mood. Intermittently she went home and continued to drink in which case she was completely inebriated when she arrived. On these occasions Patricio might send her back home. Patricio returned to Tapas after lunch, did some work, reprimanded the chef for one reason or another, then took an afternoon siesta on the wooden bench in the front lobby where I found him upon my arrival flat on his back and snoring with his arms crossed over his chest. He woke about an hour before doors opened and ate a wedge of Spanish omelet, drank a sherry then an espresso. That kept him tight until the end of the night when he sat down to eat.

Viviana drank right through the evening. She had hand signals for everything. One meant that someone's ashtray needed to be changed. Another meant that a person needed a refill. Another signal told us that a bar party was to be cashed out quickly because their table was ready. She had a signal that the bar needed to be wiped. Her favorite signal was with her thumb and index finger, letting us know that she needed a short glass of Cava, or Spanish sparkling wine. I don't understand why she didn't allow us to pour her a full glass she drank the short ones so quickly she'd easily drink a bottle of Cava during service as she played hostess. Tapas was such a party atmosphere that nobody seemed to notice or care. It didn't take long for me to notice that Vivana had a fondness for coke. Around eight o'clock each night a well-dressed Hispanic man appeared. Viviana found him a seat at the bar, gave him a glass of wine on the house and when they thought no one was looking, made the exchange. Then she would disappear into the office for about fifteen minutes before returning, somewhat sobered, smiling and signaling for another glass of Cava.

Patricio and Viviana saw themselves as celebrities. They loved walking down Boston's Newbury Street to see if anyone recognized them. I don't think anyone did. At the end of the night they sat at the big front table for dinner. Never alone they frequently invited friends and friends of friends. They loved artist types—there was a boutique owner, a wanna-be musician who played poor flamenco guitar at their table, a third rate opera singer who sang dreadful renditions of "Summertime," and a woman who was trying to be a fashion model even though she was nearly forty. Patricio and Viviana held their court. They never sat down until the dining room was officially closed so the kitchen and bar were forced to stay open for them and pity the waiter unlucky enough to draw the front section that night running around for their every last need. Viviana only picked at her dinner unable to speak a coherent sentence. Patricio ate voraciously and drank glass after glass of wine. The worst part was that Patricio didn't tip the waiter one penny. The great insult to any of the employees was that we were required to stop by the table on our way out the door and kiss Patricio and Viviana goodnight in front of their friends.

If it weren't for Lou, the waiter I'd befriended, I'd have no one to relate to. Lou was the only American on the wait staff but Patricio and Viviana treated him well. He ran a theater company they were impressed. Jorge and I were solid as a team behind the bar but culturally we had very little in common. Lou and I talked about theater, writing, art, music and pop culture. Like many of the gay men I'd worked with in the past Lou was obsessed with sex and liked nothing better than to expose his various escapades to me. Lou went through men like we went through Sangria and each day he arrived with another tale to tell.

He enjoyed sex with strangers. Often he'd meet a man at one bar, go home for sex, ditch the man and make his way out to another bar and repeat the process. It wasn't uncommon for him to have sex with three or four different men in one day. He had regulars and gave them nicknames. Shoelace Man got his handle the night he substituted a shoelace for a cock ring. During his lunch hour Drive-by drove to Lou's apartment for a quick one. Bull Durham starred in a gay softball league. Breadman drove a truck for Wonder Bread, a short, balding, chubby Italian man in his forties who lived at home with his mother. Lou liked older men, especially those with a bit of a belly. He claimed he liked to have a place to rest his head while he did his work. Lou wasn't all about sex. I found him generous, in touch with his feelings, intelligent, and brilliantly witty.

One day Lou informed me that he was leaving Tapas. His theater company had received a sizable grant and there would be enough money for him to draw a salary for a year or so. I found no one else I could take comfort in at Tapas and after Lou left for reasons I couldn't understand the waiters, always unfriendly, seemed to turn hostile. They complained to Patricio they weren't getting drinks from me fast enough and that I was developing a bad attitude with them. One of them went behind my back and said he'd seen me be rude to customers. I was wiping down the bar at the end of a long night when Patricio approached me and said he wanted to talk. He took me aside and began running down this list of complaints. There was nothing I could say or do to defend myself, once Patricio was on a roll there was no stopping him. The volume of his voice escalated with each phrase until he was screaming at the top of his lungs, banging his fist on the bar with his face turning blood red I thought he might have a heart attack. The entire crew and all of his friends at the dinner table watched.

The next day I walked in to Tapas, went into Patricio's office and gave my notice. Patricio seemed surprised, asked me why and said that I'd been with Tapas for a long time. It was as if the incident the previous night never occurred. I didn't say I was tired of his unfair bullying or his wife's bothersome nit-picking. It was time for me to move on I told him I needed something new. I worked out my two weeks and left without fanfare. On my last night I walked directly past Patricio and Viviana's table without stopping to kiss them or say goodbye. Oh Lord of Servers may I never again pour another pitcher of Sangria or hear the Gypsy Kings.

♦♦♦

Waiter!
Barkeep!
Bartender!
Excuse Me!
Server!
Garçon!

They call out loud to get my attention. I'm picking up
an order, or at a table clearing plates someone expects me to
drop what I'm doing to rush right over even if I'm not their
waiter. I can be at the other end of the bar mixing drinks and
a bar customer finishes a cocktail or bottoms out a glass of
wine and can't wait for me to finish what I'm doing—as if I can
send them another round by telepathy. The drunks are always
worst. They start working to get my attention with booze still
in their glasses, an empty in front of them unthinkable.

Wavers are particularly annoying. They wave their empty
glass in the air, or I'm across the dining room taking an order
and I see one waving their hands for me. I turn my attention
back to the table I am serving when finished I quickly walk in
the other direction pretending I didn't see the waver in the
first place. They never learn. I've had diners follow me into
the waiter station or to the bar or the credit card machine
to tell me they're waiting too long for their first or second
course, that the meal isn't up to par, that they need another
round of drinks at the table or someone is having a birthday
do we offer any kind of complimentary dessert with a candle.
It's not that these situations don't need tending to but people
invariably think that they are the only ones in the restaurant.
As if I have only one table to wait on instead of four or five
or six.

The grabbers reach out and grab. I jerk my arm or hand away to make the point, even if your table is on fire don't put your hand on me. I can be carrying dinners out or returning to the bus station with a handful of dirty dishes. I wonder what they think they can accomplish shouting or reaching out for a handful of my shirt when my arms are full.

We're still waiting for our desserts.

Could you check on our dinners it's been a while?

Could we have more coffee?

And bring more cream please.

Is this the sea bass? It doesn't look like sea bass.

I didn't think this dish was going to be like this.

It just isn't what I expected.

We're in a bit of hurry we'll order right away.

What's the specialty of the house?

I tell them as you can see my arms are full and I am preoccupied at the moment I will return momentarily. They watch me with predatory eyes until I turn my attention to them. My tip is on the line. They say it without actually saying it. As if ten percent opposed to fifteen percent will make any kind of difference in my life.

♦♦♦

I was curious when Joe Fiorino phoned me back with a slight sense of urgency in his voice. Could I come in that afternoon and talk to his wife Darlene, as they needed a server.

The previous day I made the rounds at area restaurants. The Central Bistro in Central Square, Cambridge had opened the year previous. A few servers were setting up when I arrived and one of them gave me an application but said that Darlene, co-owner and front-of-the-house manager was not in at the time.

Why didn't Darlene phone? She was the one in charge of the wait staff. I briefly turned the question over in my mind and let it go. Joe asked me to come in at two. When I arrived he explained that Darlene should be there at any moment. Five minutes later I heard him on the kitchen phone saying that he told me to come in. Joe hung up the phone, returned to the dining room said there'd been a misunderstanding and Darlene would be along in about ten minutes. In the meantime Joe invited me into his kitchen, gave me a tour of the tiny space and talked about his cooking style and philosophy. He had me taste his sauces with fresh bread he'd just taken out of the oven. I liked Joe immediately, we were the same age and he seemed like many of the kids I'd grown up with. He and Darlene had recently purchased a two family home not far from the Bistro.

The antithesis of her husband, Darlene Goldstein hailed from San Francisco, the daughter of a successful lawyer. Too young to have been part of the hippie movement, she clearly carried a tinge of the New Age in her eyes. Her hair was long and frizzy. She wore a flowered cotton dress, Birkenstock sandals and some type of mystic crystal on a necklace. We sat down at a table in the dining room and she began to talk at me in a scattershot way about the restaurant, the servers, the system, what she expected from the staff, the clientele, and taking control of our own destiny. Only take-charge people could work on her dining room floor. I said nothing; she asked me nothing. Finally when it seemed as if she were winding down I asked did I have the job. She answered yes. I asked when do I start and she said as soon as I want. I said tomorrow. She said fine.

♦♦♦

I'll never understand how people tip. I've had customers shake my hand on the way out, thanking me for the terrific service and leave fourteen percent. Others tip fifteen percent to the penny on the amount of the entire check or fifteen percent on the sub-total before tax. A few leave fifteen percent on the food and less on the bottle or bottles of wine they consume. Twenty percent is still not close to the norm. Many people begin with fifteen percent and subtract for any tiny thing they deem I've done wrong—simply to chisel a percent here and a percent there. At Tulips on large parties of six or more we add eighteen percent. I've seen people contest that while many leave extra. Tips are better on the bar by and large. Restaurant goers who prefer eating at bars tend to be more experienced and appreciate good service enough to put their money where their mouth is. Twenty to twenty-five percent is average when I work the Tulips bar.

Men usually tip better than women. No doubt this is due to the fact that they make more money than women. Teachers tip poorly. Tourists just as bad. Working class people are likely to leave a larger tip than doctors or lawyers who don't budge one extra percent. People from the south tip a straight ten percent you can keep the southern hospitality I'll never work as a waiter south of the Mason–Dixon line. Europeans are the worst. In many European countries like Italy for example, the tip is included although a little extra is left if the service is special. But Europeans who've lived here for years act as if no one clued them in and leave five percent. I like to think it balances out in the end. That there are always those who leave very gracious tips that counter the cheapskates.

Twenty-five years ago at The Greenhouse most of the

business was transacted in cash. There were no laws on the books requiring that we claim every penny. I received my small hourly waiter wage and no matter how much money I made on a given evening, I could claim twenty or thirty dollars earned. During the 1980s things changed and suddenly we had to account for eleven percent of our sales and my income dropped dramatically. As years passed more business transactions done with credit cards made it harder to hide income. Now it is a rare night when someone pays in cash so all my tips can be accounted for and I must claim one hundred percent. The income potential for servers has been reduced forever. The only place one can still hide some money is on the bar where folks pay cash for a round of drinks and bar regulars often tip cash.

◆◆◆

I never worked a restaurant as small as Central Bistro. We had no bar and got our own wine and beer stocked in the rear near the restrooms. Approximately eighteen tables filled the rectangular room, each could be moved about and against others so that a two-top could become a four-top or a four-top a six-top. There was no end to the configurations we created to accommodate diners. Reservations were recommended and on busy nights we were forced to turn away any walk-ins unless they were willing to wait but there was no place for them to stand so they huddled by the door.

Only three waiters worked on a given night. We not only served our own beverages but greeted people at the door. Servers answered the phone, took reservations, maintained a floor plan for the night, seated people and hung up their coats in a tiny closet to the rear of the place. I spent as much time taking care of these functions as I did on my waiter duties. Darlene told me she was a hands-off manager, she meant it. We hardly saw her except in the afternoon when she might be in the kitchen talking to Joe, or tasting wine with a salesperson in the dining room. Intermittently she remained for part of the evening hidden downstairs in her office. The servers were required to do all the paperwork and money handling at the end of the night. Two of us took care of the side-work the other went downstairs to the office and check by check entered the evenings transactions, balanced out the books, took out tip money and deposited cash and receipts in the safe. The system left it open for any of us to figure out some kind of cheating scam and indeed the woman that I replaced had been fired for stealing. She was especially good at figures and became the one who regularly went down to do the books. It's said she made off with hundreds before Darlene and Bob figured it out but they had no concrete proof and couldn't bring charges

We worked a set schedule and the place closed on Sundays and Mondays so it was the kind of restaurant job I could live with in terms of hours. I worked four nights per week and it was busy as word of mouth and restaurant reviews deemed us one of the hottest dining spots around. One of my weekly shifts I was required to arrive at two and man the telephone for reservations. Usually by the time the rest of the crew arrived at four we were nearly booked solid and the last openings were filled. Friday and Saturday nights were booked by mid-week, sometimes the previous weekend. Weeknights we did two, possibly two and a half turns per night and on weekends three to three and a half. The door opened and we were flat out with tasks until well after the last customers left. Considering the size of the place and the subsequent low overhead and payroll, Joe and Darlene were making good.

Joe never went to cooking school. He began working in restaurants shortly after graduating high school, washing dishes and eventually moving up to a line cook position. Eventually he found his way to the Bistro, which at that time was called Chez Philips after the owner, Seth Phillips. Seth was one of the original Boston area chefs to be taken seriously during the 1980s and responsible for the food revolution in the city that continues today. Joe began as a dishwasher for Seth, a level Seth required all his cooks to start at. In no time Joe became the sous chef, and Seth's right hand man. Five or six years the two worked side by side and by his own admission Joe learned about real cooking as Seth's assistant. Seth grew tired of the business and talked of selling, Joe decided he wanted in. With only a few investors behind him, Joe managed to raise the money he needed and fulfill the dream of owning his own place.

Because of our similar working class, Italian-American backgrounds, Joe confided in me things that he kept from other employees. One thing I learned was that Joe was a pot dealer for many years when he was younger. His activities began during high school and continued as he made his rounds at various eateries where there were always plenty of cooks and waiters looking for his product. In due course Joe quit his financial sideline, but not before he amassed a large amount of cash. Since he was never much of a party man and not greedy for material things, he rarely spent profits. He used that money when he purchased the Central Bistro. All he had to do was figure out a way to float the cash into friends' hands and use them as investors. This wasn't very difficult.

Joe and Darlene met at the Bistro when it was Chez Phillips. She worked as a waitress. They began dating not long after he became sous chef and were married about a year before they purchased the place. Joe loved the Bistro. He often referred to it as a Mom and Pop operation. It was a business that he could live with the rest of his life. Darlene had ideas of her own. She frequently complained that the place was too small, that Joe wasn't ambitious enough and that the two of them were meant for more. It wasn't uncommon to hear them arguing in the kitchen. Frequently she stormed out the back door and tore out of the parking lot in her BMW not to be seen for the rest of the day, or maybe several days. If they weren't arguing in the kitchen, they argued on the phone. I could hear Joe attempting to appease her with the phone to his ear while he prepped food. At some point he would tire of the conflict and tell her he had work to do and hang up.

◆◆◆

My least favorite part of dinner service is dessert and coffee. I greet a party, take drink orders, dinner orders, serve and clear appetizers and dinners, open a bottle wine, now I must see to it that everything's off the table down to the last of the crumbs, bring dessert menus, inform diners about the dessert specials, return for an order and begin the process all over again. People can be as fussy about desserts and coffee than they are when ordering dinner with their special wants.

Half regular and half decaf with milk.

Coffee with cream.

Black coffee but can you bring it after I eat my dessert?

Tea with honey.

Decaf espresso.

Cappuccino made with skim milk.

The dessert special with whipped cream on the side.

Peach cobbler with ginger ice cream. I don't like ginger ice cream can I substitute vanilla?

A pot of hot water for those who bring their own tea bag.

Could you ask the chef if he can make me a fresh fruit plate?

Why don't you have a cheese plate?

Their particular needs are endless. I bring the dessert order to the kitchen and explain the special requests to the cook. Then I proceed to the waiter station and begin steeping tea, steaming milk for cappuccino, pouring coffee and filling little pitchers with milk, half and half, skim milk and honey for the table. From there I make my way to the bar for after dinner drinks. Coffees and teas go the table followed by drinks, then the desserts. By the time the desserts arrive someone is ready for a coffee refill so I return to the waiter station and bring out the pot. By this time the person who didn't want dessert decides that they will have one since they look so good.

Betty Ann loves tea so we have a special tea menu featuring a dozen or so varieties of black tea, green tea, decaf teas and herbal teas. Despite the descriptions of each on the menu, invariably someone wants a verbal explanation. Each one of the teas has a specific brewing time and required amount of tea per pot. Making two or three different pots requires steps of one to three spoons, two, three, or four minutes brewing. We have timers in the waiter station we wind then the ding goes and the tea ready. The problem is timers go off while I am at the bar, clearing another table, delivering food or taking an order so that some teas are over-brewed being impossible to stand by and wait for the bells to ring with so much to do. I am called to a table and told that the tea is too strong could I bring more hot water to dilute it or make another pot. People love to linger after dinner so one after another diners signal my return to warm up their cup of coffee or bring more milk or cream.

♦♦♦

A few of the restaurants I worked were small and functioned without hostesses. As for establishments that employed hostesses I'm hard pressed to think of many that wouldn't be considered attractive. It is an unwritten rule that hostesses be young, good-looking and glamorous if possible. A hostess is the first person someone encounters when walking through the door. Who wants to see someone with a bad outfit, bad skin or bad figure? I remember one scrupulous hostess who worked at the Public Library. She came from Georgia had enormous breasts and plentiful cleavage, wore short skirts and the highest of heels. Once she asked me if John John Kennedy was in town, where might he hang out? I had no idea.

I've seen many a man dining with friends or on a date hit on a hostess. Recently at Tulips a man left with his date and after dropping her off phoned to ask Laura our hostess out. Young John the cook says he'd eat a meal on Laura's ass. It was her first day as I approached Tulips on my bicycle one afternoon and spied her out front bending over in her short skirt and spiked-heel shoes watering the flowerpots as I peddled into a parked car.

The same rule applies to cocktail waitresses. It seems as if no couple wants an overweight, unattractive woman to deliver their cocktails as they sit at a romantic table in some dimly lit corner. No group of businessmen will tolerate such an outrage. Cocktail waitresses are preyed upon. Even the shyest of men after a few rounds have a hard time resisting the urge to fall for the sexy woman walking past with a cocktail glass full of cash and a round of drinks on her tray. I see the look in his eyes. Each time she passes he looks closer and more passionate, trying to muster the courage to start a conversation. If he doesn't ask her out the first night he returns the following night and the night after that until finally he unloads the question and she delicately lets him down the way she has a hundred times. There's not a regular at a bar I've worked who hasn't fallen in love with at least one cocktail waitress, only to be rejected and find the solace he needs in his drink, playing the sad sack for a week before returning to his old self.

♦♦♦

Joe's food was simple and delicious. He favored Italian and Mediterranean influences. His soups were marvelous, especially his bisques the wild mushroom a standout. Pasta dishes were exquisite in their simplicity, homemade linguine with fresh tomatoes, spinach and New Zealand mussels. Joe liked venison—grilled tenderloin sliced and topped with a Port Wine reduction. Most sauces were reductions of one kind or another, rarely containing more than wine, stock, fruit, butter and an herb or two. Garlic and herb roasted chicken marinated for twenty-four hours before roasting. Joe loved to grill lobster on the mesquite grill that he kept fired during the night—an art form. Lobster might be served over one of his superb risottos. Joe took pride in baking his own bread. They were small loaves with a touch of cornmeal added and we served them warm with herb-flavored olive oil.

The small wait staff consisted of a few graduate students, myself, an ornery waiter named Dennis who had been the first waiter to be hired when Chez Phillips opened. Dennis commonly complained that we were lacking. A night wouldn't pass without him throwing a fit over an insignificant incident. Once on a Saturday night I threatened to take him out back and punch him in the nose after he went off on me. He never bothered me again. Craig claimed to have slept with over a thousand men. I had no reason to doubt him. We hit it off from the beginning. Craig was an excellent waiter and we shared an enthusiasm for punk and in idle moments shared adventures.

I submitted my poetry manuscript to contests and publishers but had no success. I thought I would try a small trade press located in Cambridge called Zoland Books. They previously rejected my first novel but I figured I had nothing to lose and the editor might remember my name since he wrote a supportive rejection letter. Six weeks passed and a note came in the mail. The editor said he was enjoying my book of poems and was considering it for publication. He wanted to know could he keep it for another month or so for further readings. I immediately wrote back he could keep it as long as needed. Three weeks later a letter came that he decided to publish it and could I come to his office one afternoon and work out the details. My only regret was that I had to work at the Bistro that evening and was unable to go out to celebrate. I drove to work alternating between exaltation and lament. Soon I would be the author of a published volume of poetry. And still a waiter.

With a book of poems in production my writing came to a halt. Then one morning I arose and an unexpected force drove me to my computer. The night before I dreamed of my father's gas station. I sat down and transcribed the dream as near as I could remember. Soon I found myself writing every day before going to the Bistro whether I dreamed of the gas station or not. The more I wrote the more situations I recalled from my past so that I could barely keep up. I let the work flow where it needed to go no care for a linear or chronological narrative. I wrote as if speaking to someone, allowing the language to surge as fast as my mind could recollect and record.

In several months I completed the book. I wrote it so effortlessly I figured it couldn't possibly be of value. I didn't even know what to call it—a novel, a memoir, it seemed in places more poetry than prose. I didn't think anyone could be interested in such a book—of pumping gas, car parts, mechanics, womanizing, the boy and his dad. I passed the book along to my publisher and in a matter of weeks he phoned me to say he loved it and wanted to bring it out after my book of poems. In less than a year I went from having nothing in my writing future to a book of poems and a novel forthcoming.

♦♦♦

Joe made his own desserts when I began at Central Bistro. His approach was straightforward. As the volume of business increased he was finding it more difficult to keep up with all of his tasks. He decided to hire a pastry chef part time. Jill had given up a corporate lawyer job to pursue her long time passion of cooking pastry. She'd taken a course with a French pastry Master and struck out on her own. The Central Bistro was her first position as a pastry chef. It was a disaster from the beginning. Jill never got the feel of Joe's bread recipe and her bread was uneven, adequate at best. Her desserts were over-the-top as far as Joe was concerned. Everything looked as if she were trying to match something on the cover of *Gourmet*. Joe wanted an approach that complemented his food, not upstage it. He liked cobblers, bread puddings, and simple cakes. Jill found all of this pedestrian. Joe tried reasoning with her but she was more concerned about her image and what kind of desserts she wanted to be known for. Joe let her go.

Stan played guitar for many years working as a journeyman in the restaurant business. He'd been a line cook, sous chef, and pastry chef. Stan brought no recipes of his own, instead made any dessert that Joe requested and did it well. He perfected Joe's bread in no time. During the 1970s Stan had been a sideman with several semi-big acts including Muddy Waters. Stan did a solid job of burning himself out on drugs and booze eventually left the music world and never looked back. He reminisced about those years but claimed he no longer owned an instrument nor the desire to pick one up again. He listened to classic rock stations and sang along. Stan liked talking to himself in the kitchen alone. Occasionally his conversations got violent.

I'll punch you in the fucking face.

I'll rip your heart out.

I'll kill you and cut you up into pieces.

Don't look at me that way I'll mess you up.

I'll smash your fucking head in.

How would you like me to rip your eyeball out?

Women servers were afraid of him Joe insisted that Stan was harmless and only had a few screws loose. Stan always seemed lucid and able to maintain a conversation and liked to smile. He drove a twenty-year-old wreck, lived alone in a tiny apartment in Allston and never went out except to work. He claimed to spend free time watching television and loved reruns of old situation comedies. Stan's desserts were delicious, consistent, and he worked as hard as any kitchen worker can.

Darlene paid a guru to learn about things like astral projection and polarity. She preached about the benefits of such practices and encouraged us to pursue them. She could spend hours in her office in the dark, staring at a lit candle. If I knocked on the door and inquired about how to deal with a certain situation she'd say handle it without looking up from the flame. We were required to make intentions at the beginning of every shift. She kept a sheet posted in the waiter station and with each of our names we had to intend a certain amount of covers we would do that night. If we only intended fifty, she said, we would only do fifty. If we intended seventy-five, we would do seventy-five. She insisted that we controlled our destinies. We all placated her and intended as high a number as possible.

As Darlene began to take more of an interest in the place her presence increased. In between her sermons on polarity she took to criticizing us. This was puzzling since we were a small, experienced crew and service and side-work were never lacking. Her harping was never about anything specific or constructive, mostly that some people didn't care or do enough of one thing or another. She continued to carp on Joe that he wasn't ambitious enough and they needed a bigger place and other restaurants not nearly as deserving as Central Bistro were getting way too much exposure in the press. She went from the kitchen to the waiter station even in the dining room she complained to customers she couldn't accommodate the amount of people who wanted to come to the Bistro they needed a bigger place. Unless she pointed her disapproval at my work I tuned her out.

In due course Darlene and Joe hired a public relations person—an upstart yuppie who drove a brand new sporty Saab and walked into the Bistro as if she owned the city. The first thing you know Joe and Darlene got a makeover. If they were going to be celebrities they must look the part. Joe and Darlene spent several afternoons on Newbury Street getting stylish haircuts and buying overpriced clothes. In a matter of a week Darlene went from a ragged, frizzy-haired hippy to a stylish cosmopolitan who jelled her hair and wore make-up I'd heard her denounce countless times in the past. She began wearing evening dresses, dark stockings and heels. Joe who never wore anything but jeans, t-shirts and sneakers had his mullet cut to a short, jelled hairdo and began wearing dress shirts, slacks and Italian shoes to work before changing into his kitchen whites. Shortly after that Darlene traded her BMW for a Mercedes and Joe traded his old pick-up truck for a brand new SUV.

♦♦♦

This is my last night on the bar at Tulips. Tomorrow night I work on the floor and finish out my time. Business is moderate tonight. Several bar regulars wish me luck. I no longer resent their needs—the special requests, for tastes of wine we serve by the glass, extra bread without butter but could I get them some olive oil from the kitchen. These tasks suddenly seem effortless and painless. They'll miss me and when I make it to the big time, say I remember him when. I've heard it all before. I smile. Could be.

The bar regulars want the atmosphere of a city place without having to go into the city. They are lawyers, scientists, computer people, a group of women doing a girls night out, an occasional couple meeting for the first time from an on-line dating service. These types of folks are cordial, not too over friendly until they get a few into them. I've known many regulars for the seven years I have been here.

The dining room drink orders flow in: lots of glasses of merlot and chardonnay, Cosmopolitans and Vodka Martinis made with designer vodkas, single malt scotches and vintage ports after dinner, a few beers. I do the usual banter with the waiters, tease Tiger the vintage will change by the time he picks up the wine, he says he's slow to pick up drinks because it takes me forever to make them. I feel I'm having fun—the way I haven't for a long time. Maybe this isn't so bad.

Even if I find work how will I ever match the income of this business? But I think of the schedule—weekend nights, weddings, showers and anniversary parties on Sunday afternoons. Saying goodbye to my wife and daughters on these days or afternoons during the week, missing dinner and evenings with them. Not to mention the physical ailments. The bunion that has been growing steadily on my right foot begins throbbing an hour into my shift I swallow over the counter painkillers and walk on the right side of the foot. The way my lower back and legs ache in the morning. How I look in the bar mirror crows feet around the eyes, gray beard and gray hair working with servers younger and younger with the passing of each year, stylish haircuts, tattoos, lip and eye rings. I make myself another espresso, my third of the night. No matter how many I consume it doesn't relieve my fatigue. If not now, when?

♦♦♦

Keep Watching the Sky appeared in April of 1996. That May I began at Tulips and the following September Zoland Books brought out *Gas Station*. To everyone's surprise the novel received fantastic reviews from small literary magazines to *Publisher's Weekly* and *The New York Times*. As a result I experienced a tremendous shot in the arm. During this time Molly and I were in the process of adopting our first daughter, Julia Gan. Excited about the prospect of becoming a parent, I also feared the responsibility would likely put an end to my writing. The financial and time burdens I imagined would leave me little energy for literary pursuits.

I worried unnecessarily. The day after we returned from China in December, I began writing another novel with Julia Gan harnessed to me at the computer. Over the next three years I wrote three novels. Zoland Books was committed to my work but during production of my next novel, we came to an editorial disagreement. My editor Roland Pease wanted me to use a fictional name instead of calling the city Somerville—otherwise he wouldn't bring out the book. I lost my book deal and publisher.

Then one day out of the blue an English publisher contacted me. I had never heard of Gollancz Books. I made a few inquiries to friends and learned that they had quite a reputation in the literary world. It seems a young editor with the company had picked up a copy of *Gas Station* in a foreign bookstore in London. He loved it. When he found out I had unpublished novels stacked up he asked to read them. To my surprise, Gollancz bought the rights to all of the books and over the next four years brought out four of my novels including an English edition of *Gas Station*. I made little money on the deal but the books were well reviewed in England and had a life there though never distributed here in the United States. Thus I lived a life of a writer and a servant by night.

♦♦♦

Public relations paid off. Suddenly Darlene and Joe's pictures were appearing in all the newspapers. Joe's recipes were included in seasonal cooking articles. *The Boston Globe* even ran a feature on the couple one Sunday. Small local papers got in on the act with photos and stories on their success. Rave reviews rolled in from all corners. We were booked nearly two weeks ahead for Friday and Saturday nights and weeknights several days in advance. Everyone wanted to eat there as it goes when any restaurant becomes the latest trend.

The moment the doors opened to well after last seating we moved as fast as possible, seating people, hanging coats, attending to our own bussing as Darlene still insisted there was no need for bus people in such a small place. Bottles of medium to expensive wines were flying out. Darlene increased the wine menu prices by thirty percent and no one seemed to care. The kitchen pumped out food as fast as possible. Joe kept the crew small one sous chef and one person making salads and desserts. The food did not lack and Joe kept an amazing consistency. A young woman named Martha from El Salvador washed dishes and pans five nights per week. Next to Sammy at Tulips she's the greatest dishwasher I've ever seen. She didn't miss a beat and I never heard anyone in the kitchen call for pans, nor were we ever out of glasses and silverware.

Despite the continued success Darlene was not happy. She complained about business being turned away and said she and Joe needed a bigger place. Worse, she spent more time at the Bistro, complained about our lack of attention to side-work, not greeting people at the door fast enough, not stocking wines on the shelves in the wine room properly. Her erroneous denouncements took their toll. One particularly busy Saturday night, one of those nights when everything seems to go wrong, she was especially harsh on Craig. She followed him around the dining room into the waiter station and kitchen bitching endlessly about nothing. Craig already had his fill of her and finally ran angrily into the kitchen where Joe was overwhelmed with orders and handed his apron to Joe. He said he was leaving right then and there. Joe asked why and Craig said he simply could no longer work for Joe's wife. Craig walked out the back door and never returned.

This event did little to curb Darlene's behavior. In some ways it got worse as she acted misunderstood, she told Joe Craig was a primadonna and called a mandatory wait staff meeting for the following Saturday afternoon. Right from the start it was clear that we were there to be berated. Darlene said that no one was above her and that each and every one of us had improving to do. She read from a list of infractions that she'd witnessed committed by all of us over the past months and grew angrier as she read so that she was yelling by the end. If we didn't like it, there were plenty of people out there who would love to work at Central Bistro. At the close of the meeting our morale was at an all time low. Several of us talked of handing in our notices that night. I decided to hold off and think it over. The following week Darlene seemed to rein in her tirades. Perhaps Joe had talked with her. But it wasn't long before she was up to her old tactics. I had my fill. One day I walked in when Darlene wasn't there and gave my notice to Joe. He pleaded with me to reconsider; my mind was made up.

◆ ◆ ◆

All my years in the business I only waited on a handful of famous people. Most places I worked were simply not located in the "in crowd" areas. I remember waiting on actor Dana Andrews at The Public Library. I recognized him because my mother had a crush on him and I got his autograph for her. Mr. Andrews looked older than I imagined. It wasn't long after that I heard he passed away. A young John Kerry came into The Public Library lounge, sometimes with a younger woman. Boston Celtic Robert Parish also frequented the lounge for a while, he too with a younger woman. Boston news personality Liz Walker, a beautiful tall black woman arrived for drinks along with another attractive woman.

My fondest memories of celebrity waiting were at the Boylston Bistro. I waited on comedian Richard Lewis and his wife. I remember being struck by how short he was. He seemed tired and I could tell he wanted to be left alone. Ted Kennedy dined with a woman and drank several screwdrivers before switching over to wine with dinner. He looked older and fatter than on television. My greatest moment at the Bistro was the evening *Happy Day's* Scott Baio dined and was nothing less than the most arrogant little prick. Loud and contentious, unsatisfied with the menu he insisted that all he wanted was a steak. He wanted a steak, couldn't I just get him a plain fucking steak instead of all this shit food. Half the people in the dining room turned and stared. Serge picked up on the ruckus. I told him what Chachi said about the menu and he became outraged. Serge had already put away several drinks that evening, so had Tim. Serge went downstairs to the walk-in fridge and pulled out a sirloin. By the time I brought the steak to the table Serge had put it up his ass-crack and Tim had spit all over it. After a few minutes I walked to the table to see how the celebrity was enjoying his steak. Fine, just fine now can you leave us alone? This entree became known as the Chachi steak.

At Central Bistro I waited on the great alto saxophonist Benny Carter in town to receive an honorary award from Harvard. Sweet gentleman Benny sipped beer and politely put up with the Harvard music department types who tried to act hip with him. At one point one of the female professors put her arm through his and began to come on "Oh Benny" she said like a little girl, "I think we're trading fours."

I also waited on young up and coming rock stars that the folks at WBCN would bring in. I remember one particular young woman everyone doted over. So strung out she ordered a bowl of soup and nearly feel asleep staring into it, never so much tasting a spoonful. The doctor and novelist Robin Cook was a regular at the Bistro. Darlene and Joe treated him like royalty whenever the senior citizen came in with his child bride. We were under instructions to accommodate him whenever he called, or arrived unannounced wishing to sit at the best table by the window. A person obviously used to being around servants he treated us as if we were part of the woodwork. Once I was waiting on him Darlene came over and mentioned that I wrote and he never even looked up from his bisque.

At Tulips I waited on Anita Hill who was lecturing at Harvard—gracious and beautiful. Several pop artists made Tulips a regular stop on their way or returning from a hot new recording studio in Acton. One night I waited on Natalie Merchant and Billy Bragg they seemed like an item. Another night the poet Seamus Heaney came in for dinner. One evening academic Henry Louis Gates left me an eight percent tip. I waited on conductor Ben Zander, a pretentious, obnoxious, entitled person. If anyone ever deserved a Chachi steak, he did.

At Trattoria Napoli Julia Child walked in. A long-time resident of the neighborhood, I turned to see her tall frame at the front door, in her nineties and frail, walking slowly to the place that Gianni quickly set for her at the best table he could arrange. He determined that he would wait on her then called me into the waiter station to command me not to mention the wild boar or venison special while she was in the restaurant. She was pleased with her meal, although she told Gianni the homemade chicken soup needed more salt. He later admonished the chef to no end, humiliating him in front of us all, how could a chef send out unsalted soup to Julia Child? Gianni had his picture taken with Julia, and he had it blown up and hung it in the front window with the rave reviews.

◆◆◆

Trattoria Napoli was the only job I ever found through a newspaper ad. I should have known better. Up to then most jobs I held came from word of mouth, a friend, my own instincts and footwork. I always wanted to work in a real Italian restaurant and never had. At first visit Trattoria Napoli resembled any of the Trattorias I'd enjoyed in Italy. The owner who interviewed me described the food as authentic as anything in Italy and one of the only real Italian restaurants in the Boston area. It was a small square dining room with red-brick walls exposed kitchen and tile floor seating maybe forty people. Gianni said he and his partner Roberto, both of whom were from Naples and spoke English with accents, spent one hundred thousand dollars renovating and updating from the country French place that served that part of Cambridge for fifteen years. During the interview Gianni asked was I hungry. I answered that I could always eat. He told the chef to fix us some pasta and in no time the chef appeared with two bowls of linguine and clams with garlic and olive oil. It tasted just like in Italy, or better, the way my mother prepared the dish.

Trattoria Napoli sat in the heart of a part of Cambridge known to locals as The Quad. A small quadrangle of real estate outside of Harvard University and Harvard Square—and one of the wealthiest areas, block for block, in eastern Massachusetts. Denizens of The Quad were mostly folks from old New England money and a few upper crust Harvard administrators and faculty. I heard of houses with thousand dollar doorknobs. Quad folks thought themselves a cut above the rest, I sensed in how they talked down to me. These were seasoned travelers. The food at Trattoria Napoli reminded them of the memorable meals they'd eaten in Italy.

The initial downside to my employment at Trattoria Napoli meant working lunches. The place opened for lunch Monday through Friday and I had to work two shifts. I was hesitant on my interview but when Gianni told me how much money I could average on my night shifts, I sold myself out. They did a cash business, no charge cards accepted and I could claim the minimum amount of tips for tax records, the rest would be under the table. They were looking for a workhorse, someone to do five and six nights per week. I told Gianni I was a writer, I needed time to write and I could do three nights per week including two doubles. If necessary I would work an occasional fourth night. He didn't seem satisfied with this, but offered me the position anyway providing I could do extra nights until he hired another part-timer to fill in the gaps. Only one other waiter worked there at the present time—a homely Sicilian, a gambler who worked seven days a week always in debt. Gianni and Roberto waited table as well. Gianni said they didn't always take a full cut of the tips. They'd take a hundred-fifty while I'd make two hundred. It sounded okay to me.

Gianni and Roberto pushed us to sell the specials. The regular menu was simple and reasonably priced but the owners weren't satisfied with selling clams with linguine. They preferred selling the special linguine with mussels, clams, shrimp and whatever other shellfish or seafood they had that particular day. This dish nearly doubled the price of the linguine with clams. The same could be said for the veal chop, grilled or the special stuffed with a tiny bit of cheese and prosciutto, at nearly double the price. There were at least seven or eight special entrees every night and several appetizer specials. Don't forget sell the specials Gianni and Roberto constantly reminded me. I was scolded when unsuccessful and the customers who ordered off the menu were ridiculed behind their back. They also pushed what they referred to as their homemade ravioli, salmon filled, lobster filled, wild mushroom filled, none of which were homemade but purchased elsewhere and kept in the freezer. These dishes were overpriced. The same was true for wine. There was a wine list but if someone ordered a bottle we informed them that for a few dollars more we had a special Italian wine no one else had.

In spite of this I carried on. In no time I made more money per dinner shift than ever before. Each night before we opened the specials got posted on a blackboard in the kitchen. I did my best to keep them all in my head, we mentioned them orally and without talking price. Rarely did diners inquire about the special prices. The Quad folks simply paid their bills, another medium priced meal out for them. Folks that did enquire about prices of specials generally ordered off the menu. The ones who failed to ask but should have were often stunned when the bill arrived. Those people never came back but Roberto and Gianni didn't seem to care. Their philosophy was to make as much money as soon as they could. The future didn't enter into the picture.

Two weeks into my employment my old friend from Tapas, Lou, appeared to inquire about the other waiter position. He was on his way to rehearsal. I told him there was something fishy about the place that I couldn't quite finger yet, but the money was great and we could make a schedule that worked for both of us. Gianni inquired about Lou after he left, I told him Lou was as good as a waiter gets. Gianni asked me does he steal. I told him of course not. Gianni hired Lou and soon I had the schedule I wanted and was working with someone I liked. Shortly after Lou started Gianni took me aside and with his accent asked me about Lou's sexual preference. Roberto and Gianni had nicknamed me Peppe, short for Giuseppe. It sounded more authentic than Joe.

Peppe I have a to aska you someding.

Sure.

Thisa Lou. Heeza gay?

Why are you asking me?

It'sa nodat I care. I jus a wanna know.

Why don't you ask him? Because I'ma aska you. It'sa no madda me. Roberto wanna know.

Well then Roberto should ask. What difference does it make?

It's a nonna my biz. Butta Roberto, he's a little, you know …

I don't know. And if you are concerned, ask him yourself.

From that time on Gianni and Roberto never treated Lou the same way. They made childish innuendos that Lou shrugged off. Behind Lou's back they were crueler, and intimidated. It was clear that had they known Lou was gay they never would have hired him. Neither one of them could understand what would make a man be like that. Lou was uncomfortable. He was waiting for some old restaurant friends to open their new place in Arlington where he would go and take the position of bar manager. So he bade his time. It would be a good place for me to wait table he said and I kept it in the back of my mind.

◆◆◆

Three special restaurant days make true amateur events: New Year's Eve, Valentine's Day, and Mothers Day. The worst of the three is Mothers Day, forever commemorated on a Sunday in May. It's a money-grabbing day. Tulips is open from noon until nine in the evening. We need at least an hour or more to set up which means arriving at about 10:30 in the morning and by the time of night cleanup it is eleven and makes for a grueling shift. Reservations roll in about ten days in advance and starting a few days before the phone doesn't stop ringing. By Sunday we are booked full, but groups of five or six or eight still walk in without a reservation and phone calls continue throughout the day.

New Year's Eve and Valentine's Day at least mark times for celebration, Mothers Day is like a duty. Countless families arrive, with as many as three generations at one table, in-laws mixed together the mood is inevitably somber at best. Punk rock teenagers and college kids forced to dine with the family carry pusses that reach down to the table. Tension between siblings or parents and children is thick and rises from the tables like heat off asphalt. Folks shout across tables at grandmothers deaf, near death, their heads bobbing from some kind of neurological disorder, do you want a drink? Brandy Alexanders are the rage. Because of the amount of large parties we must accommodate, several parties are disgruntled over the location of their seats. Hour in and hour out we turn tables, reset and the next wave of Cleavers arrives.

It is a good day for the kitchen to keep it simple but raise the prices. Most families, especially older members, avoid cream sauces, garlic flans, or skate. Prime rib, sirloin steak, mashed-potatoes, baked Cod, chowder, green salads are good fair for the day. The kind of food the chef and cooks can prepare and put out with their eyes shut. The worst food complaint might be a return on a prime rib to be cooked up to well done. Uncomplicated desserts like bread pudding, a chocolate cake or apple-crisp works fine. By the time dinner is cleared, folks can't get out fast enough and don't want dessert. But someone at the table insists that grandma order one, and they wait tapping their fingers or feet, heads bowed, sipping a second cup of coffee as grandma eats one bite per minute too polite not to finish. The father signals for the check so that there will be no time to waste when grandma's through. Fortunate thing for me I am able to add eighteen percent gratuity to each check, otherwise who knows how low the tip could go?

New Year's Eve is a night of tremendous anticipation, for silly resolutions of discontinuing habits, losing weight, reordering finances. The celebration is a night for people to believe that they've had a remarkable time, done something special, let it all hang out. Over the years the night isn't what it used to be with heightened sensitivity towards driving drunk and substance abuse people have kept it closer to home but I remember one particular New Year's Eve at The Public Library where at one in the morning I was serving dinner and could barely make my way through the chaos and noise of the dining room. Diners shouted in my ear, blowing horns and shaking rattlers, women stopped me and kissed me on the lips. People danced around the room making a chain that grew longer and longer. The line into the bathrooms ran out the door as people vied for stalls to snort cocaine. Some unknown force drove everyone.

By midnight things are slowing down. Many dinners have gone out and the last of the desserts are being served. We still hand out party favors and pour free champagne as the big hour nears, but the noise and pitch of drunkenness is checked. Perhaps the hardy partiers no longer go out and opt to make merry at a house party where they might stay over in order to party to their hearts' content. No matter, the craving to mark the passing of the night, to do something special—no matter how hard they try, is always disappointing. New Year's Day nothing has changed. The official end of the holiday season leaves emptiness.

New Year's Eve the fair includes lobster, rack of lamb, wild mushroom ravioli, homemade rolls, exotic salads and appetizers, mousses and roulades. The price-fix is high and the diners demanding. Service must be impeccable, expensive bottles of wine and champagne flow. Tips are generally good and follow suit with the inflated menu prices. But the night is long and the three or four turns take their toll by the time the last customer leaves by one o'clock and I'm exhausted before cleanup. The only thing that keeps me going is a shot of something in my coffee, then champagne, several glasses of it. The kitchen crew puts out leftover food and we eat. By three in the morning tips are counted up, the waiter stations and dining room clean, I make my way home, tired and dazed. Upon arriving I am too wired to sleep until five or six in the morning.

I wake with a mild hangover, legs and back aching, and limp through the first day of the year.

Valentine's Day is another night of obligation. Guys who need to keep, repair, or improve standings in their relationships know well to make use of this Hallmark night. Large parties are non-existent on Valentine's Day. Tables for two begin booking a week or more in advance but late calls come. The men sound desperate, perhaps they forgot until the last minute—or maybe they had no intention of making plans until they learn their girlfriends or wives fully expect a special evening. No matter, utter disappointment when they learn they are too late.

Women inevitably wear the sexiest red dresses they can squeeze into. Cleavage and black stockings rule the evening. The power of perfume overcomes the garlic and spices wafting from the kitchen. Champagne is the drink of choice, hand fondling common, and more than one marriage proposal can be expected during the course of the night. The tears flow as the bride-to-be tries her diamond on, and I must be enthusiastic and congratulatory, as does the manager and hostess, thankful that he chose our place to pop the question. More than once I've had couples break up on this the night for lovers. Raised voices and cries, followed by a woman running out on her own, a man left raising his hand for the check. It is a dreadful sight to see. Check averages are high and tips are better when men paying think that they will be getting laid. This confidence lubricates their wallets. It is a long night but lovers are easy to please.

◆◆◆

Gianni was bald except for a thin row of hair on each side of his head. He had a pointed hooknose and black shark eyes.

Gianni prefaced everything he said with I have to be honest with you. I have to be honest with you I only married my wife so I could get a green card. I have to be honest with you if I don't get laid every day I have to jerk off two or three times to relieve the pressure. I have to be honest with you the tips weren't very good tonight. It was a cash business and at the end of the night Gianni or Roberto took the money drawer downstairs and returned with our tips. They added up the checks made deductions and divided the rest for us. If Gianni and or Roberto worked as waiters they took a cut for themselves. Usually the money was very good, but now and again an evening's tip-take seemed particularly low.

If an attractive woman came to dine, Gianni couldn't think of anything else. He walked around like a caged animal, unable to concentrate. First he insisted on waiting on the table so he could flirt, regardless of whether the woman was with a date or husband. Then he continually found his way to the table to make small talk and preen over the fact that this was his restaurant, how much of a success it was, how the food was so authentic some times if he forgot a recipe he would phone his mother in Naples to get it. He had a series of sayings he repeated. Walking back and forth from the table into the kitchen.

Whatta fuckin' tits on her.

I give it to her very bad.

Believe me if she no with him I getta her number.

She's a know she driva me crazy.

I betta her pussy smell like breath offa da baby.

I fucka her so hard my dicka come outta her mout.

On the surface Roberto acted more civilized. Married with three children he owned a pricey home in nearby Winchester. In time I learned that he was as sleazy as Gianni.

He boasted of ripping customers off when he and Gianni worked in the North End. They added additional items on checks and pocketed the difference. During their days most restaurant transactions were still done with cash. If a customer brought the addition to their attention, one of them apologized and said they got some checks crossed. Mostly people never noticed and the two of them could double their take each night. Roberto often retold an anecdote of the time a man pulled out a roll of hundreds to pay his bill. One bill fell to the floor and the customer didn't see it. Roberto put his foot over it and said good night to the man walking away.

Working a busy evening at Trattoria Napoli was complete chaos with no system to speak of, like traffic in Naples. We were supposed to take tables in turns but Roberto and Gianni constantly threw a wrench into things by claiming a table they could bilk a lot of money out of and soon they would be yelling that Lou and I weren't keeping up. They seated people in so tight that there was no place to move in the dining room. Carrying dinners out, clearing plates became nearly impossible. We accepted reservations though hardly honored them. The phone rang on Saturdays and they would just keep taking names. There was no place for people to wait inside the tiny dining room so by eight o'clock waiting lines stretched down the street and around a corner. Occasionally someone would come in and tell Gianni that they have a reservation. Signor, he would say, everybody out there has a reservation.

Around two months into my stint at the Trattoria, things began to unravel. I learned that Gianni and Roberto operated at levels beyond just bait and switch on the menu and wine list. Regular menu items and bottles of wine on the list were practically off-limits for us to sell. If we were unable to discourage a diner from any of these items, we were told to inform them that we were out of it that day. Wines by the glass were available, and mostly we sold house wine or Chianti at about five or six dollars a glass. One night a woman ordered a glass of vintage Barbaresco that sold for twenty dollars. I removed the bottle for the rack and took it into the waiter station to open. Gianni saw me and ran up excitedly.

Peppe, whatta you open da Barbaresco for?

Because the woman on table eight ordered a glass.

Whatta you crazy?

What do you mean?

You givva dem dis?

Gianni proceeded to pour a glass of house red. I told him that was unacceptable, the woman would know.

Day don't know nothing.

Of course they do. Besides, I won't serve her that.

Gianni said if I won't he will. He walked over the table, placed the glass of wine delicately down with a smile.

Here's a you Barbaresco.

The woman thanked him and Gianni returned warning me off opening an expensive bottle of wine that we serve by the glass on the list. I still insisted that the woman would know. Further, I told him that was too unethical and I refused to do it.

Etical? Whatta you crazy? Iffa somebody order it you calla me and I give it to dem.

He waited until the woman had taken several sips of the wine. Then he walked over to the table and bent over.

Excussa me, Signora, how do like a da Barbaresco?

Oh, it's delicious.

He returned to the waiter station.

Pepe, Deeza people, day don't know a fuckin a ting, believe a me.

The next day I phoned Lou, now the bar manager at a

new restaurant in Arlington. He said the place was just getting off the ground in terms of business, and they had all the staff they needed at the present time. If I could hang in there a while, there would surely be some openings in the not so distant future.

Meat and produce were kept in a locked refrigerator in the basement that was off limits to everyone except the chef, Gianni and Roberto. One morning I came in early to set up for lunch. I went to the basement to get some supplies and noticed that the lock on the door had been left unlocked the night before. Curious, I opened the door and went inside to have a look. Immediately I sensed things weren't quite right. I noticed there were a dozen or so pork loins in vacuum-sealed packs. Funny, we didn't serve any pork loin. In a plastic container I saw what appeared to be more pork loins marinating in red wine. Could this be the wild boar marinated in Barolo wine we served for twenty-five dollars? Then I saw several leg-cuts of beef, also vacuum packed. Another container held several of them marinating in wine. The only beef we served was the sirloin on the regular menu that were kept in the freezer and defrosted in the microwave if someone ever ordered one. The leg-cuts were the venison we served, smothered in a raisin sauce of some kind. I couldn't believe that Gianni and Roberto were getting away with it. Further, fabulous reviews rolled in about Trattoria Napoli, from newspapers to spots on local television shows. It was all too much.

The espresso beans were kept in a five-gallon plastic bucket. One day I walked down to the basement to catch Gianni mixing cheap bulk coffee beans with the espresso beans. Suddenly I realized why the espresso sucked at the Trattoria. I thought it was the machine. Gianni and Roberto didn't believe in decaf espresso. If someone ordered one they simply ran the drip through used grounds and served it as decaf espresso. They kept a half-full can of ground beans in a Decaf Lavazza can in case anyone should question. They kept a pasta maker in case someone should ask about the ravioli and pasta they boasted about but purchased elsewhere. There was no end to their scheming. One Saturday afternoon we served a private party. The people brought their own Italian rum cake for dessert. Gianni and Roberto charged a plate fee, fair enough, and for some reason the clients left the remainder of the cake behind. Gianni and Roberto sold slices of it as the dessert special that night.

Then there was the prosciutto. Every two weeks prosciutto was delivered by truck from New York City. The delivery truck carried only prosciutto, destined for places like Providence, Philadelphia, and Portsmouth and Portland. A phone call came in from the driver about an hour away. No one except for Gianni or Roberto accepted the prosciutto. When the call came we had to track down one of the owners if they weren't present. It seemed strange to me that in a city like Boston with all the purveyors available, Gianni and Roberto purchased their prosciutto from New York. I did the math and couldn't understand how a company in New York City could make money paying for a truck and driver to drive to various states only to deliver a few prosciuttos. Gianni and Roberto claimed it to be special prosciutto that wasn't available here. Upon arrival they took it immediately downstairs. Once I caught them in the basement, Gianni, Roberto and the driver, surrounding the table on which a prosciutto lay. They jumped up because I surprised them. Gianni said they were removing the tag, that all the prosciuttos had a tag with a number to make certain it was authentic. I never did find out what was inside those prosciuttos, it seemed much ado for a quarter of a pig.

I reached the end of my limits when I confirmed what I had suspected all along. Gianni and Roberto were stealing tips from me and the other waiter. We began keeping track of the evening's take. One night we were certain we had cleared over two hundred each. After doing the books Gianni handed us one-seventy. We confronted him and he flatly denied cheating us. In fact, he took offense at the accusation. We told him this wasn't the first time we'd kept track and he said we made a mistake. I received a phone call from Lou just about that time. There was an opening at Tulips and he could get me a position there. I immediately gave my notice. Gianni and Roberto were insulted.

People I knew booked a special dinner at the Trattoria. I pulled Gianni aside. If everything wasn't on the up and up I told him, I would contact every place from the Cambridge Chamber of Commerce to newspapers big and small. Gianni said he didn't know what I was talking about. I then told him I knew everything, from the specials' scam to the espresso beans and wines by the glass. He denied it all right to my face and said that they would never do anything like that. I warned him again that I knew, and so did Lou who had many connections in the business—any problems with my friends and he and Roberto were finished. Gianni and Roberto didn't speak a word to me as I worked out my notice. They were not present my last three nights and only appeared at the end of the shift to count out the money, as they always did. To this day people line up out the door to eat at Trattoria Napoli, and the front window is plastered with numerous ecstatic reviews.

♦♦♦

My last waiter shift passes quickly and painlessly. Business is moderate. I do my end of shift side-work and it seems less an effort than in the past. Lou's working the bar and asks would I like a drink. No. The other servers and I do our paperwork, then combine our tips and divide them up. Not a bad night's take. Especially since we are finished at eleven. I say goodbye and shake hands with the newcomers who I don't know too well. Lou and I embrace and promise to have lunch soon. I hug Barb who I have been working with since I first began at Tulips seven years ago. She tells me not to be a stranger.

Outside is Indian summer. Leaves turn. Here and there they fall, and the sweet smell of early autumn decay. I pedal my bike down Mass. Ave. Traffic is modest, the cars that pass, I catch up to at red lights, pass them and then they pass me again when their light turns green. Once the flow goes by everything is quiet. I have no idea where I am headed, what the future holds. Images of working as an all night shelf stocker, a cab driver or variety store clerk cross my mind. I know that I must remain out of the business no matter what it takes. Something is out there for me. Standing on bike pedals to stretch my legs I feel like I am floating.